WITCH
QUICK

MIDLIFE IN MOSSWOOD BOOK 4

louisa west romance

GET WITCH QUICK

MIDLIFE IN MOSSWOOD BOOK 4

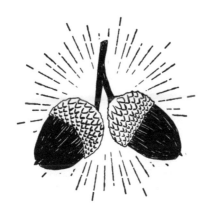

LOUISA WEST

Edited by Kimberly Jaye

Proofread by Lindsay Aggiss

Cover design by Louisa West

For Elizabeth - my own Pumpkin.

The magic is inside you. There ain't no crystal ball.

— DOLLY PARTON

CHAPTER 1

"Whoa, nelly!"

Ben darted backwards, holding up his hands, as he nearly collided with a large piece of thick plywood being carried by two sweating volunteers. People swarmed Lee Park, carrying tables and chairs, or pushing trolleys, or carrying boxes full of a delightful assortment of what could only be described as *stuff*.

Ben stood for a moment, still as a tree, and then spoke in the sort of voice a tree might use if it surprised itself by suddenly speaking.

"Did I just say 'whoa, nelly?'" he asked the air.

One of the movers of plywood snorted at Ben's existential crisis. "Sorry," he added. "Didn't see you there."

"No harm, no foul." Ben took up his roots and moved toward Rosie and the quartet of folding card tables she was setting up under a tree. Various plants covered the tables around her, giving off an urban jungle vibe, and she was unpacking even more greenery from boxes that were sitting on the grass.

"And 'no direction', apparently," Rosie murmured under her breath, with a nod at the retreating lumber. The men carrying it paused before a petite woman with a clipboard, and a blonde ponytail that looked like it belonged on *I Dream of Jeannie*. She knocked on the wood as though the two guys holding it were just as dense, and then pointed angrily clear across the park.

"Prissy's in fine form," Ben agreed. "I don't know how she managed to talk Carol-Ann into lettin' her be on the Fair Committee, but I *do* know she's being a real pain in Tammy's—"

"*There* you are," Rosie said loudly to Maggie, who had just arrived. Ben coughed uncomfortably, saved from his faux pas. Wide eyed and out of breath from running wild with the other kids, Maggie struggled to talk but it didn't stop her.

"Mom," Maggie huffed, oblivious. "Some of the other kids are going down to Fortescue's for a bit. Can I go too? *Please*," she added hastily. Rosie pursed her lips. Now that Randy was out of their lives for good, she'd been trying to let Maggie have a little more independence... but she wasn't sure it extended to letting her daughter go for ice cream with a bunch of kids and zero adult supervision. Plus, they had work to do.

"Have you finished setting up your fair table?" Rosie asked, even though she knew the answer.

"Can't I just do it in the morning?" Maggie asked. "It won't take that long."

"If it won't take long then you can do it now, Pumpkin," Rosie said pointedly.

During the course of this discussion, a small girl with dark eyes and a pointed chin had dashed up to stand by Maggie's side—no doubt to play the part of moral support. Rosie's reply made both girls groan. Maggie heaved a sigh and threw a look at her friend, who shrugged helplessly and took off in search of the other kids.

"Mo-ooom," Maggie added after the girl had gone. "No 'Pumpkins' in public, remember?"

Rosie bit the inside of her lip, feeling a little guilt nipping at her heels. It seemed to her like she was always in a balancing act between being a mom who adored her kid and being a mom who had an almost-teen on her hands. She remembered reading an article once that warned against the dangers of your teens coming to see you as their friend instead of their parent. But... surely you could be both. Right? Rosie let out a slow breath, pushing the guilt away.

She glanced at Ben. He pressed his lips together to hide his smirk, and began to help Rosie with her plants.

"These look amazing," he told her, hefting a chipped but charming pot of Zinnias onto a table. "If you weren't opening Nourish soon, you could sell these in

3

the Go-Go. Folks'll just love the whimsical touches," he added, nodding at a small plastic bee on an almost invisible wire stalk that poked up between the blooms.

Rosie smiled, happy to be distracted from Stern Mom duties for a bit. She considered the bee fondly, and then turned the pot she had just put down so that the shabby-chic streaks of rainbow-colored paint were displayed to best advantage.

"Well thanks," she said, a warm glow of pride warming her cheeks. She had been working hard in the greenhouse for months to prepare for the Mosswood Easter Fair. Her old nemesis, Craigslist, had become her new best friend, and she had scoured local advertisements for free garden items that she could repurpose into her own brand of pre-loved nature art. The bee was just an eccentric button from an old sweater, and the pot had been rejuvenated with old paint. Combining the art with the plants Rosie could cultivate with her magic allowed her to create something special. She only hoped everyone else felt the same.

Pausing for a moment, she popped her hands on her hips and nodded in the direction of a large white marquee not far away. A swarm of people were setting up a makeshift counter out of plastic trestle tables, and two long gas griddles were sitting off to the side awaiting orders. "How's everything going with the PPA kitchen?"

Ben grinned. The Pineview Progress Association

would be raising money to keep up the plantation house owned by the original founder of Mosswood, which was now owned by the town itself and was its crowning jewel.

"'Bout as good as it can be," he said, "when everyone involved has strong opinions about which type of mustard should go on the hot dogs, or which brand of sweet tea we need to serve them with."

Rosie grinned too, and the pair of them watched Maude Merriweather from the Beep'n Sleep pointing animatedly at a ketchup bottle someone else had just put on the counter next to the controversial mustard.

"You'd better go and break up that brawl," Rosie warned him. "Maude looks ready to get physical."

Ben sighed melodramatically. "You're right. Later Rosie. Bye Maggie!"

"Bye," Maggie said sullenly, turning her table the right way up and plonking an empty plastic tub for her candy underneath it. "There," she announced to her mother. "Done. *Now* can I go hang out with my friends?"

Rosie took a deep breath and turned her gaze on her daughter. Seemed like she was going to have this little showdown whether she wanted to or not. "Have you asked any adults I trust to go with you to keep an eye on you?"

Maggie's shoulders sank. "No."

"So, you didn't finish your chores before asking and

you didn't get a grown up to go with you. I think you already know the answer."

Maggie's face was a darkening thundercloud. She crossed her arms over her stomach. "You never let me do anything fun," she murmured under her breath.

Rosie tried desperately not to roll her eyes. This child was going to ruin her last nerve.

"It isn't my fault you made the choices you did. Maybe next time you'll make different choices and be able to go get ice cream with your friends."

"Incoming!"

Rosie was distracted from her increasingly moody child by a rosy-cheeked Tammy bustling across the grass towards their stall. She carried a big plastic tub and wore a smile, despite the sweat beading on her brow. Myles wasn't far behind her, following in the wake of Tammy's flowing floral dress. Something that looked like a huge piece of cardboard wrapped in brown paper was tucked awkwardly under one of his arms, while the other guided it through the crowd like a rudder.

"You just missed Ben," Rosie announced, sizing up the mysterious package while clearing a space on the table so that Tammy could put down her box. "Is that what I think it is?"

Tammy beamed. "Sure is," she gushed, almost dancing on the spot as Myles set it down to lean against the table. "I know you're just dyin' to see it, but if we open it now—"

"—we'll lose the element of surprise," Rosie agreed with a nod that made her trademark ponytail bob. "Best leave it wrapped for the big reveal tomorrow! Hi Myles," she added with an apologetic smile, before frowning slightly. "Where's Declan? I thought he was supposed to be helping you guys?"

"He's bringing the last tub of stuff over from the car," Tammy explained with a distracted wave in the direction they'd just come from before she started pulling more tablecloths and a bunch of paper plates, bowls, and cups out of her tub. It looked as though she intended to feed the whole of Mosswood and then some, and Rosie felt relieved that everything was going to plan.

And then she spotted Declan.

Just once she wished that she could experience a fantasy the way they played out in the movies, where the crowd magically parted for the hero so that he was in full, glorious view the whole time for maximum perving potential. But that was *not* the way things worked for Rosie.

She felt the familiar haze of admiration drift over her as she saw Declan trying to push his way through small clusters of people, gripping the sides of a tub that was twice as large—and apparently twice as heavy—as the one Tammy had carried. His biceps bulged with the effort, and she could see the dark patches of sweat already beginning to dampen the chest and underarms of the navy blue polo shirt that set his red hair off just perfectly. He looked *pissed*, and she saw him mouth something that might have been 'By all means, let *me* get out of *your* way, ya witless git' as he tried to make his way over.

Actually, maybe this was better than a stock-standard movie-replay. He looked hot, sweaty, and bothered, and she wouldn't have minded seeing whether she could use that energy to her advantage. He looked up as he got closer and caught her staring; his mossy green gaze locked onto her face and just when she thought he might be even more annoyed that she was witnessing his supreme efforts to not lose his shit, he smirked.

Tammy, who was *not* perving on her boyfriend in that exact moment, managed to clear another space for Declan to put his tub down. Rosie blinked once the spell was broken, and then handed out bottles of cold water she'd popped in her cooler earlier that day.

A chorus of thanks echoed through their small assembly, and they spoke briefly about the few things that had happened since they had all been separated only hours beforehand. And then the real work began. Rosie finished setting up her plants while Maggie helped Tammy lay out the rest of the tables and the chairs they had managed to commandeer from everyone's houses.

Myles spread the cute, kitschy tablecloths over each and placed a plain glass milk bottle in the middle as a centerpiece, just waiting for Rosie's green thumb to give them the perfect finishing touches the following morning. Declan was building the stands for the string lights that would drape across their 'restaurant' area, and Rosie joined him to place little vines she had cultivated in the pots that served as a base. Once everyone else had left for the night, she would send her magic to the vines and they would creep up to cover the wires of the string lights for a magical, fairyland effect that would eventually be the living porch of their actual store.

"Everythin' looks amazing, love," Declan told her, stepping down from his ladder and pulling her into a sweaty hug. She wrinkled her nose and pretended not to like it. She knew it was a huge cliché and she would never have admitted it out loud, but there was just something about the way he smelled that drove her wild.

"Thanks," she said after a deep sigh that had very little to do with relief at nearly being done getting ready for the Fair and everything to do with Maggie, who was still sulky (but thankfully not being rude to her Aunt Tammy).

"You okay?" Declan pulled back, scanning her face with concern. "You seem a little off."

"It's just been a long day is all," she told him, with a quick but meaningful glance in Maggie's direction. He followed her gaze and then his eyes cut back to her before he nodded in understanding.

"A hot candlelit bath and a good night's sleep'll soon set you right," he promised softly, leaning in to kiss her temple before he moved to install the next stand.

Declan was right—that sounded heavenly. Rosie kept the thought of such a lovely reward in the front of her mind as they all finished doing as much as *could* be done the night before the big event that would hopefully double as the successful launch of a new business.

"Reckon that about does it," Myles said with a proud smile, brushing his hands down the front of his jeans. His thick, dark hair seemed almost jet black in the fading light of the afternoon, but his blue eyes were bright and alert. "Teamwork makes the dream work!"

Tammy looked pleased as punch, and quite like she would have enjoyed giving Myles a bit of a cuddle now that the work was done but she clasped her hands in front of herself instead, as though afraid they might wander if she didn't keep them under control.

"See y'all in the mornin'," she beamed instead, slipping her purse strap up onto her shoulder.

"Bright eyed and bushy-tailed," Rosie promised with an answering smile. She slipped one hand into Declan's and half-turned to Maggie, who would normally grab her other hand. This time however, Maggie stepped past her mother to take the lead. Rosie glanced at her own hand, feeling a blush creep into her cheeks as her daughter moved on without her. Maggie probably *was* getting too old to hold hands while walking, but for her part Rosie could have kept up the habit for life. She straightened up her shoulders, pushed the thought away, and turned back to say goodbye to her friends.

Maggie reached the truck first and leaned against the side of it with her arms crossed while she waited for her grownups. Declan unlocked it, and they all climbed inside and got themselves situated.

They passed the public library, the last of the afternoon sun drenching the stretch of grass beside it that ran down to the river. A group of kids were gathered around a park bench. Some were sitting, some standing; others had bikes or scooters. Rosie glanced at them horsing around, noting that the streetlights had already beamed into life.

Maggie kept her eyes on them as the truck drove past. When she could no longer look over her shoulder, she turned to look through the windshield ahead with a blank expression.

CHAPTER 2

After a fitful sleep, Rosie woke the next morning to the unmistakable smell of coffee and toast. The gentle, rhythmic snoring to her left told her that it wasn't Declan who had gotten up before their alarm to prepare breakfast. Her heart swelled with love for a moment, before regret let the air out of the balloon. She sat up in bed slowly, leaned over to press a feathery kiss to the top of Declan's shoulder, and then dragged herself out of bed.

Maggie was in the kitchen, carefully buttering hot toast. A small smile crept onto Rosie's face as she stepped into the light of the room, noticing the quiet darkness of the world outside. Maggie heard her approach, turned, and then looked crestfallen.

"It was meant to be a surprise."

Rosie folded her into a hug, biting back a sigh. "It *is* a surprise," she said, smoothing Maggie's bed-ruffled hair. "A lovely one. Breakfast in bed sounds wonderful on a day that's set to be so busy. Like the calm before a storm."

"I'm sorry for everything yesterday," Maggie said quietly, sounding like she might well be on the verge of tears. Rosie knew her daughter like the back of her hand, and Maggie's olive-branch-breakfast didn't cancel out the depth of emotion that was lying beneath the surface. She didn't want them to fight today. There was so much riding on her and Tammy making a good impression with their store, and she didn't have enough time to sit down and talk properly about things just now. Declan would be up any minute, and they would be wolfing down coffee and toast before heading down to the park to make their last-minute preparations.

It was Executive Mom-Decision time.

"Thank you," she murmured back, leaning down to kiss Maggie's cheek. "I appreciate you saying so, and breakfast looks lovely." She plucked a piece of toast from the stack on the counter and took a big bite. "Yum."

"Okay," Maggie said, already sounding perkier. "I'll go wake up Declan to let him know breakfast is ready."

"Great idea," Rosie said, pouring the fresh coffee.

The next half hour passed in a blur of eating, dressing, and the brushing of teeth as well as the packing of final items into the truck. Rosie carried the last plant—a small cement pot hosting long tendrils of creeping fig—down the porch steps as the sun began to peek through the branches of Needlepoint Woods. And that's when she saw the biggest damn rabbit she had ever seen in her life.

It was enormous, and the kind of snowy white that made it seem almost incandescent. It looked at her balefully from next to the front tire of Declan's truck, its eyes shining with an ethereal red sheen in the light from the porch. Rosie was just slowly starting to put down her plant so that she could reach into the back pocket of her jeans for her phone to get a picture when Maggie came skipping down the porch steps behind her.

The startled rabbit took off in leaps and bounds, melting into the grey murkiness of the pre-dawn landscape. Rosie blinked and then turned her head towards Maggie, who was almost already at the truck.

"Did you see that?"

"See what?" Maggie asked, whirling to face her mother in the manner of a kid who was at risk of missing out on something cool.

Declan locked up the house, and then jingled his keys in his hand out of habit as he stopped by Rosie's side. He glanced in the direction Rosie was looking— towards the woods. "What is it we're 'sposed to be lookin' at, love?"

"Nothing," Rosie shrugged, hefting her plant and peering into the woods again before heading for the truck. "I just need a bucket full of coffee is all."

They rattled through the half-lit woods that marched right up to the sides of the access road to Fox Cottage.

The headlights on the truck roamed through the underbrush like searchlights, leaping ahead of them through the darkness the way that giant rabbit had bounded across her lawn. It was probably someone's pet that had escaped, Rosie reasoned as she relaxed against the soft leather seat next to Declan.

Maggie had taken to wanting to sit by the window, which suited Rosie just fine. It was the best of both worlds. Maggie got to entertain herself by watching the world slip by, and *she* got to enjoy how delicious her boyfriend's cologne smelled. She glanced sideways at him now, admiring his strong arms and the way he casually gripped the steering wheel.

Yum.

"What's that?" Maggie asked as they came out of the woods and onto the steadily declining road that would see them onto the highway.

"Hmm?" Rosie asked absently, turning to look at her daughter.

"Down there," Maggie pointed, levelling her hand at a section of the road towards the bottom of The Ridge where the old sugar and syrup mill sat on the corner of the highway.

"Hayes?" Declan asked, confused. "You've seen it a million times, wee'an."

"No," Maggie insisted. "Look at the road!"

Rosie squinted. Now that Maggie had pointed it out, there *did* seem to be something weird on the road. It was almost like a white haze spread across the gravel, stretching from the sugar mill on the right to the start of the woods on the left.

Maggie sat up straighter with excitement. "Is it *snow?*"

"Don't be silly, it's nearly summer," Rosie said, straining her eyes for a better look. And that's when she noticed that the haze seemed to be *moving.* In small, measured little hopping motions.

"What the—" Declan breathed, slowing the truck down to a crawl.

An army of snowy white rabbits confronted them. Their beady little eyes lit up red like thousands of beacons in the light from the truck's headlights. Declan hit the brakes, rolling them to a total standstill.

"Whoa," Maggie breathed, shuffling forward so that she could see them better.

"What in the *world?*" Rosie asked, exchanging a puzzled look with Declan.

"That old saying about doin' certain things like rabbits looks like it's been taken a bit too literally," he remarked, winding down his window. He leaned out of it, attempting to shoo the rabbits away with vigorous gestures, but they all just stared at him as though he was a maniac.

Maggie turned to him with interest. "What things?"

"Never you mind," Rosie intervened, an eyebrow cocked as she turned to survey their situation. There were rabbits as far as she could see—all the way down the hill to the highway.

Rosie had never seen so many rabbits in one place before. She'd been willing to bet that *one* white rabbit on her lawn was an escaped pet from town, but there was simply no way thousands of white rabbits had escaped—except maybe from a laboratory of some kind. That had to be it. Surely?

She began to gather her arcane energy with a view to at least clearing the road if nothing else. They had a Fair to get to, and she wasn't about to concede defeat to a throng of long-eared fluff-balls. Focusing her intent on just shuffling the rabbits off the road, Rosie stretched a hand out towards the windshield and slowly released her magic in a gentle stream.

Each of the rabbits lifted their heads high as they felt the soft wave of magic flow over them, ears held straight up in the air. But then, as the magic subsided, they all started to dash around madly. They zipped across the road like white flashes of lightning, kicking up gravel and zig-zagging through the grass.

The magic had moved them, alright. Just not the way Rosie had intended. She heard Declan mutter something under his breath to her left.

"We're gonna have to walk," she declared, gesturing to Maggie to open the door. They didn't really have that much to carry, and if they waited for a clear road then they would likely still be there later that night. Rabbits covered the road behind them, hopping up the hill towards Fox Cottage. The sun was almost up.

"Not like we have any other options," Declan

agreed, flinging open his door and startling even more rabbits into action. "What the hell is going on in this town?"

"Who knows?" Rosie replied, sliding across the bench seat as Maggie let herself out of the truck first. "I mean, bikers and crazed dark witches, and evil Sheriffs? Of *course* a plague of white rabbits is the next logical conclusion."

They set off down the road towards the highway. Rosie carried her plant securely on her hip as though it were a baby, while Maggie toted bags of the candy she had made with her Aunt Tammy in the lead up to the Fair. Declan carried everything else with ease, and if it hadn't been for the fact that they all needed to watch where they were going to avoid falling on their face or stepping in rabbit poop, Rosie would have really enjoyed the view overall.

They passed Hayes. The windows were covered outside with old metal security mesh, the glass inside each and every one broken by the weather or by well-aimed rocks. The building usually gave Rosie the creeps, but it was hard to feel weird about it when it had been taken hostage by a sea of white rabbits.

Maggie had been quiet the whole walk down The Ridge. She carried her candy bags carefully as though her goods might get damaged otherwise. She watched the rabbits with interest, taking note of how they interacted with each other; leapfrogging their companions and eating the sweet spring grass. Rosie started to ask her if she was okay and then thought better of it, Maggie's accusation of being treated like a baby echoing in her mind.

It wasn't a short walk, but it was one that Rosie had usually done at least twice a day since her arrival in Mosswood—dropping Maggie at school, working her shifts at the Go-Go Mart, or ferrying laundry back and forth to the Kwik Kleen. The trio plodded across the quiet highway and onto the left side of the road, which would eventually become Mosswood's Main Street.

If they had been expecting the rabbits to thin out any, then they were to be disappointed. The highway was just as full as the cottage road had been, and it looked as though the infestation spread clear all the way into town. They were just nearing the Beep'n Sleep— the small garage-slash-motel Declan had spent some time staying at in the Fall—when the grizzled voice of its owner rang out through the warm, early morning air.

"This here's a chicken coop *not* a rabbit hutch, ya pesky powder-puffs! Vamoose!"

As they got closer to the single gas pump that stood watch outside of Maude Merriweather's office they could see the elderly woman in denim dungarees and a sun hat trying to escort rabbits out of the somewhat luxurious hen-house Declan had built for the rag-tag flock of adopted chickens she lovingly called The Dames. She waved her arms, knocked off her sun hat accidentally, and then saw Rosie, Maggie, and Declan approaching.

"Well, aren't you three a sight for sore eyes," she puffed, leaning back with her hands on her hips to catch her breath a minute. Her short, curly grey hair was stuck to her forehead with sweat from her efforts. "Declan— be a doll and chase those rabbits out of the coop, would you please? They're eatin' up all the fruit I put in there for The Dames' breakfast!"

A small smile of amusement and appreciation flickered across Rosie's lips as Declan dutifully set down his bundle of stuff and went to the rescue of Maude's hens.

"Where do you 'spose they came from?" Rosie asked Maude conversationally.

Maude tilted her head in a matter-of-fact manner, her eyebrows raised. "Ain't no tellin'," she said slowly. "Not really. Maybe a rabbit farm truck overturned up the highway a ways. Though why they'd be truckin' live rabbits is anyone's guess, poor critters. People think just cos they're bred for eatin' that they don't deserve comfort. Disgraceful!"

The way the Beep'n Sleep had been built next to the local vet clinic was no coincidence. Maude was a well-known animal lover and local wildlife carer, who was forever taking on animals that needed rehabilitation or a temporary home.

"We're just on our way to the Fair," Maggie said, brightly.

Rosie glanced at her before looking back at Maude. "Would have thought you'd be down there already, helping the Progress Association serve their breakfast."

"Lord no," Maude said quickly with a comical shake of her head. "Ben Major runs that kitchen like Gordon Ramsay, and there's only so much orderin' around you can take once you get to my age. No ma'am, that man is better off left to run his own show on Fair day."

Maude sounded gruff, but there was a distinct twinkle in her eye when she spoke about Ben and Rosie knew that her boss had a soft spot for the elderly woman, too.

"Well, you're welcome to walk down with us if you'd like," Rosie added, watching Declan scoot a rabbit out of the chicken coop. "I don't know that there's gonna be any other way to get there. We had to leave the truck up on The Ridge."

Maude started to bend down to retrieve her sun hat, but Maggie stepped forward to do it for her. Maude smiled at her.

"Thanks, missy. I'd love to join y'all, if you're sure I wouldn't be in the way?"

"Wouldn't ask if you would be," Rosie grinned, which earned her a grin in return.

"I'll just get my purse while the Rabbit Whisperer over there finishes up," Maude announced, stepping into her small but neat office.

Meanwhile, Declan was hunting down the last rabbit in the hen house. He had to duck low to avoid hitting his head on the roof while he stalked it, his arms wide and his mossy green gaze trained on it intently. It huddled in the corner of the coop, and when he was a few feet away from it, he pounced. Emerging from the coop triumphantly with the rabbit held aloft in one big hand, he closed the door carefully behind him.

But his victory was short-lived. The rabbit struggled in his grip and managed to reach around to nip him on one of his fingers.

"Ah!" he exclaimed. He dropped the creature, which skittered away into the mass of other rabbits.

"Are you okay?" Rosie and Maggie asked in unison, both moving closer to try and check the finger he was inspecting.

"I'm fine. Little bugger didn't break the skin, thankfully." He paused, looking first at Rosie and then at Maggie. "But I'm the luckiest guy in the world to have you both so concerned for me." He pulled them both into a quick family-style hug, which Rosie melted into and Maggie playfully attempted to escape from. The clearing of Maude's throat brought a sharp end to their impromptu public display of affection.

THEY SET OFF DOWN THE ROAD TOGETHER, PASSING Granny's Diner as they came into Main Street. The sun was up by now, and the town was abuzz with other people who had woken up expecting the excitement of the annual Easter Fair only to be greeted with a different type of excitement altogether. Rabbits filled the town, nibbling on the carefully curated spring plants in the Main Street planter boxes and bringing traffic in the whole of Mosswood to a standstill. Folks gathered in small, concerned groups, whispering about the strange situation as rabbits loped around their feet without a care in the world.

"Glad it's not just an issue out our way," Rosie murmured quietly as she leaned towards Declan.

"But it's a bigger issue than we'd like," he countered back in a whisper. "No natural rabbit is resistant to your kind of magic."

Shit. She hated to admit it, but he was right. A new line of worry etched itself into her brain, flowing thicker with each thought that fed into it. How had the rabbits not been affected by her repelling spell?

"Thanks for that," she whispered back to him sarcastically. Declan shrugged.

Maude spoke in passing to almost everyone who was on the street, highlighting the fact that she was a staple of the community whether she was keen on the idea or not. Maggie seemed to just be taking it all in; her eyes wide and her grip still tightly concentrated on her bags of candy.

They reached the end of Main Street and turned left to look into Lee Park, which was on the right side of the street across from the Town Hall where the eventful Harvest Festival had been held.

Rosie gasped as the scene unfolded before them.

People were running and screaming—flapping their arms, waving broomsticks, and using anything else they could get their hands on—to try and shoo the rabbits away.

The bright green grass of the park was almost completely white with snowy fur. A rabbit sat happily on a table nearby, munching on the pages of some flyers that had been put on display. One rabbit dashed through the crowd, a lollipop stick clamped in its mouth as it made off with its unusual bounty.

And then something terrible dawned on Rosie.

She clutched her plant closely and broke into a stilted run towards the area where they had set up their stall. It was no easy feat, leaping rabbits and avoiding humans alike, and when she got to her destination Rosie wasn't entirely sure that it had been a good idea in the first place.

The stall that had aimed at launching Nourish into the world had been completely and utterly trashed. Rosie's plants had all been knocked over, the lush plants themselves nibbled down to tiny, sad stumps. Tammy's beautiful vintage lace tablecloths had been partly dragged from the tables, their delicate edges dirty and frayed. Maggie's candy table had been knocked over entirely.

Rosie felt her determination starting to drain out of her, disappearing like water out of a bucket with a hole in it as she placed her creeping fig plant on the ground at her feet. Her shoulders sagged and she surveyed the scene with a feeling of utter helplessness. She let out a long, shaky breath, but before she could take another one she noticed a lone rabbit still sitting on one of the tables, staring at her defiantly.

Oh hell no.

Gritting her teeth, Rosie lifted her shoulders and opened her hands in anticipation. She took a couple of painstakingly slow steps in the direction of the rabbit, looking like a more deranged version of Indiana Jones in *Raiders of the Lost Ark* as he tried to swap a solid-gold Incan idol for a sandbag. When she judged that she was close enough to make good, Rosie lunged for the bunny.

She felt the smooth fluffiness of its fur slide through her grip, and she struggled to tighten her fingers without hurting the critter. But he was too fast, and too wily, and too damn *silky* to be captured so easily. He flew through the air like he had been shot out of a cannon, landing on the grass several feet away. And as he streaked away and lost himself in the crowd, Rosie was less disappointed in herself for failing to catch him and more concerned about the magical energy she had felt covering his fluffy coat.

A magical energy that felt *very* familiar to her.

At that moment, Declan and Maggie arrived at the scene. Rosie's gaze went immediately to her daughter, one brow held high in an expression of innate motherly knowing. Maggie looked around the destruction with horror, her candy bags held limply, and then turned away quickly when Rosie caught her eye.

Busted.

"This is absolutely bloody *manic*," Declan declared, plonking the rest of the stuff they had brought with them down with relief before stretching his arms and hands to get the blood flowing to them again.

"It's cancelled, is what it is," Carol-Ann announced, wandering over from the stall next to them. "Sorry folks." Her slightly wrinkled face was trapped in a downward slope of disappointment, her shoulders stooped in a way that made her look much older than she was. "Fair's over. We need to work out where these darn rabbits came from, and then send them back there ASAP."

A growing sense of dread began to bubble up inside of Rosie. It was like the horror of a toilet backing up when there wasn't a plunger for miles. But they couldn't just stand there and watch. They had to catch this rising tide of sewage water before it spread any damn further. She turned to Declan, grabbing his arm and pulling him close.

"We need to fix this," she whispered urgently. "*Now!*"

Declan huffed a nervous laugh. "How? It's not like we can use magic on them, is it?"

"So, we don't *use* magic," Rosie snapped, trying desperately to keep her cool as she dug her cell out of her back pocket. She dialed Tammy's number.

It took several moments for her friend to answer, but when she did it was with the usual enthusiasm and warmth Rosie had come to expect from the cheerful, determined woman.

"Hello—Tammy speaking," she chirped, and Rosie almost smiled. It was such a relief to hear Tammy's voice, and she hated that she was calling with bad news.

"Hey—it's me," she said.

"Hey me," Tammy replied, registering the tone of Rosie's voice. "What's wrong?"

Rosie hesitated, and then took the plunge. "You haven't been outside today, have you?"

It was Tammy's turn to hesitate. "No," she said slowly, as though any number of disastrous possibilities were running through her head. "Why? What's happened? The weather's fine, I can see that glorious sunshine through my kitchen window."

Rosie could hear her friend's footsteps echoing on her polished ceramic tiles as she walked in the direction of what Rosie could only presume was her front door.

"Tammy, don't—"

"Aaaaagh—no!" Tammy yelped. "No, you don't! No!" There was a loud bang that sounded like a front door being slammed shut. Rosie winced as the noise assaulted her ear and held her cell aloft for a second.

"Tammy?" she called into her phone. Eventually the sound of the phone moving and Tammy's beleaguered voice came through the speaker.

"*I'll be right there.*"

CHAPTER 3

I t took *hours*. They ferried their boxes to the curb over the span of several trips. Feet were dragged, hands and knees were scuffed, and they seemed mere shadows of the humans they had been when they had set out for the Fair earlier that day. Rosie was absolutely exhausted, and it felt like this day was never going to end. She kept her eyes on the prize; the growing pile of caught rabbits on the curb.

By the time they were on their last trip, Rosie noticed that news crews were setting up on the fringes of the action. It must have taken them ages to get into town, much less right up to Lee Park; multiple vans with lights and microphone booms were poised to corral the hapless citizens of Mosswood into making countrified comments on camera ready for their prime-time news bites.

Rosie turned to hurry Maggie up as they neared their

finish line, only to see that one of the reporters had drawn her in.

"How old are you, Maggie?" the news reporter asked, leaning down to smile at her.

"Ten," she replied, wide-eyed as she stared at the camera focused on her. In the background of the shot people were trying to net rabbits, or carry them, or jump over the darn things as they raced through the park.

"And what do you think of the rabbits?"

"Well," Maggie drawled, as though she was unsure what to say, before excitement took over her features. "I think they're pretty awesome, even though they cancelled the Fair. They're so white and fluffy— they look just like Easter rabbits!"

The reporter laughed. "You're not wrong there, Maggie! It looks like Easter has come early to Mosswood, folks—there's no telling where these rabbits came from, but at least some *bunny* is happy to have them in town. This is Alex Greene for Channel 4 News. Back to you, Samantha!"

There was something other than pure, childish excitement over a town full of rabbits in Maggie's eyes. Rosie watched her daughter steadily until she recognized the expression.

Pride.

Her suspicions confirmed, Rosie scooted forward to grab Maggie's hand, dragging her out of the immediate vicinity of the news crews. "Maggie! You can't go talking to news stations!"

"Why not?" Maggie challenged. "She asked me to!"

"Because I said so!" Rosie started, but as soon as she heard the words come out of her mouth, she took a breath and started again. "Because you're too young, for one, and because you're the *reason* they're here in the first place!" Rosie sighed and glared at the reporter. "They're supposed to have my permission before talking to you, anyway."

Maggie huffed. "I'm your kid, not your *property*," she grumbled.

Rosie looked at her sharply.

"I'm gonna make your iPad *my property* if you don't lose the attitude and start helping with these rabbits."

Maggie was silent, chin lifted defiantly. Rosie glowered back.

"You can't just load them into my car!" Ben yelped, passing Rosie and Maggie on the sidewalk. He followed a score of people who had multiple rabbits stuffed into pet carriers and cardboard boxes with breathing holes hastily poked into them.

"Yours is the only car that's *here*," someone pointed out. "No one else could get close! Open the trunk, Major."

Ben pursed his lips as though he was about to say no. He looked across at Rosie helplessly.

"Why don't you bring them on up to the Cottage until we can find a shelter that can take them, Ben," Rosie offered. She leaned closer in toward Ben and tried to mumble without moving her lips. "The abbits-ray are agical-may."

Ben's eyes widened. He pressed the button on his car keys to pop his trunk, and raised his voice over the din of confusion. "Uh, yeah, bring 'em over here! I'll take 'em on up to Fox Cottage. Rabbits this way!"

"Okay," Declan said dubiously, scratching at the rust-colored scruff on his jaw. "How're we gonna do this?"

What had been expected to be a lazy afternoon basking in the glory of a soft opening for Nourish had become a war council meeting at Fox Cottage. A mountain of boxes and containers bearing rabbits was piled high in the middle of the back yard.

"I dunno, man," Ben said with a sideways glance at Declan. "That's a *lot* of rabbits."

He wasn't wrong. Rosie was still looking at the wall of boxes, plastic tubs, pet carriers, and anything else people had found that had been big enough to hold a rabbit or two. They formed an unsteady wall across the back lawn, teetering every time a rabbit skittered inside. It *was* a lot of rabbits, and as she surveyed the situation Rosie could feel herself getting mad all over again at Maggie—who was still denying any involvement whatsoever.

Breathe, girl, Rosie told herself. *First deal with the rabbits. Then deal with your unruly offspring.*

"We can't leave 'em like that," Tammy said, taking the words right out of Rosie's mouth. She threw her friend a grateful look.

"Tammy's right," she agreed. "Those boxes aren't humane, so we need a better temporary solution."

"And we haven't even caught all the rascals," Myles interjected. "The churchyard's still full of 'em. People will be rounding 'em up out of their yards for days."

"My car already smells so bad," Ben lamented, earning him a sympathetic pat on the shoulder from Declan.

Rosie sighed. "Alright. We need a better place to keep them."

She wandered over to the opposite side of the yard, closer to the line of trees that marked the beginning of Needlepoint Woods, gathering her arcane energy as she walked. She kicked off her shoes so that she could feel the earth under her feet, marveling as she always did about the amplification it gave her magic. Declan and Maggie had moved to flank her wordlessly, standing just behind her as she sank to her knees in the soft, spring grass.

Taking a deep breath as though bracing herself to dive into a pool, Rosie sank her fingertips into the soil in front of her. She felt the roots of the grass brushing against her skin, feeling the hypergrowth that came from nature during this time of year. She harnessed that growth, coaxing it towards her. She called to the trees of the woods, begging them for their assistance, and slowly released her magic in a long, steady stream of conscious desire.

Before long, tender vines began to poke up through the ground. The vines soon became branches, drawing gasps and whistles from the non-magical onlookers as they realized that Rosie had called forth the roots of the nearby pine trees. She felt Declan and Maggie pushing their magic through her like a channel, assisting with the task so that she wouldn't be drained at its conclusion.

The roots began to twist up to form a long, braided fence, not unlike the way bees form a honeycomb. Each shape fit snugly with the next, and the one after it, and so on—leaving no room for wily rabbits to hop, dig, or squeeze their way out of. It formed a round pen, with two branches winding themselves into an intricately wrought wooden gate.

Rosie let her magic dwindle and turned to thank both Maggie and Declan for their help. With her hands on her hips for support, she nodded at the rabbits on the other side of the lawn.

Everyone started moving the rabbits into the pen, keeping the gate closed and opening the boxes and such over the side. Ben returned with his second box, and froze.

"Uh, guys?" He turned to look at the crew, his eyes wide. "Are they escaping? Please tell me I'm not the only one who can't see any rabbits in that pen?"

"It's an invisibility spell," Declan assured him, clapping a hand on Ben's shoulder. "Lean over the fence."

Ben threw Declan a dubious look, before he rested his box on top of the fence and unlatched it. The rabbits inside leapt into the air and then dashed to their short-lived freedom. Ben leaned into the pen as they flew out of the box, watching them wildly scramble off and then huddling together with the others on the far side of the pen indignantly once they realized they'd been duped.

Ben leaned back and blinked when he could no longer see any rabbits at all.

"That's a trip."

He turned to Rosie. "You *do* know that rabbits breed like... well. *Rabbits,* right?"

Rosie shrugged.

"Whatever they get up to inside that pen is the next guy's problem," she decided.

IT HAD BEEN A LONG-ASS DAY, FILLED WITH excitement, aggravation, and exertion. When Declan had offered to make dinner, Rosie had managed a grateful 'Yes please!' before skipping off to de-bunny in the shower. They all sat down to a meal that consisted of colcannon—one of Declan's Irish favorites that really just seemed like a fancy version of mashed potato to Rosie—and perfectly cooked steaks. Rosie found her enjoyment of an easy evening overshadowed by the impending conversation she was going to have to have with her daughter about the sudden appearance of hundreds of magical rabbits.

Maggie wasn't stupid. She had likely known that she would be caught out. But she was also stubborn as a mule. Rosie's light attempts to get her to come clean throughout the afternoon had all come up empty, and now it was time to bring out the big guns.

"Magnolia," she began, reaching for her wine glass. "Is there anything you would like to talk about?"

Rosie watched Maggie's head snap upwards at the use of her full name, a spark of fear in her eyes. "I don't think so," she said slowly, a little *too* lightly, and with a hefty display of faux-innocence.

Rosie sipped her wine. She took her time, letting the tension in the air steep. The longer she waited, the more uncomfortable Maggie looked. "How interesting," she added at last, but her tone made it clear that Maggie wasn't off the hook just yet. "I would have thought you'd use this opportunity to apologize for flooding the county with giant white rabbits."

Maggie clutched her fork, her nostrils flaring in an expression that was slightly rabbit-like itself. "I didn't have anything to do with it!" she said quickly. Realizing that she wasn't likely to get anywhere with convincing her mother, Maggie turned to appeal to Declan. "I promise!"

"Maggie," he said softly, eyes downcast as he laid

his knife and fork aside. "You know that magic comes from within the witch that creates it. An' because of that, it leaves a kind of aura. We can tell the difference between magic conjured by ya Mum, and magic that's come from you."

Rosie was grateful for the back-up. She looked from Declan to Maggie and shook her head slightly. Who was this little cub with teeth, and what had she done with mama bear's precious angel?

Maggie opened her mouth as though she were going to protest her innocence again, but she decided to switch tacks at the last second.

"I didn't mean to! All I wanted to do was to have a rabbit around the place for Easter—a big ol' white fluffy one, like a *real* Easter Bunny! And then when my magic came out, it sort've just..." She held her hands out in front of her, opening her fists in an explosion gesture while blowing a wet-sounding raspberry.

"You can't just do magic whenever you want to!" Rosie scolded. "It's *dangerous*. Look at all the trouble you caused—not to mention the cancelling of the Fair!"

"*I didn't mean to,*" Maggie repeated, her cheeks getting pinker by the second. "It was an accident! Just like your accident with the Christmas tree, Mom!"

Wow. Maggie's timely reminder of Rosie's own magical mishap hit her right in the guts and knocked all the wind out of her sails. Rosie was partly shocked by the audacity of her child and partly desperately trying to find a reason why they weren't the same thing. She grasped at the first straw.

"And as soon as I knew I had messed up, I asked Declan—someone much more magically experienced than I am—for help!" Rosie shot back, her frustration fraying the edges of her voice.

"Well maybe that means that *you* shouldn't just be doing magic whenever you want to, either!" Maggie huffed.

Rosie's brows shot up. "I'm a grown-up," she said, even though she didn't *feel* it now. "And I'm able to make judgement calls that you're not capable of making at ten years old, Magnolia."

Maggie clenched her teeth. "I'm not a baby! I'll never learn to make decisions if you don't let me *try!*"

"Deciding *not* to get a grown-up after you released a plague of rabbits on Mosswood is not a good example to use right now," Rosie warned.

Sensing that the conversation was sliding into a definite downward spiral, Declan levelled a serious look at Maggie. "What do you think your Mum would've done if she'd accidentally exploded rabbits all over the place?"

The question had the desired effect. Maggie stopped shooting sass at her mother long enough to consider herself, and Rosie fortified herself with another sip of wine. In the few seconds that passed, the tempo of the discussion seemed to slacken off.

"She would've gotten help," Maggie admitted

begrudgingly. She heaved a sigh and glanced briefly at her mom with eyes that suddenly brimmed with tears. Then she leaned forward on the table, resting her head on her arms and tucking her face away so neither of them could see her cry.

They had finally reached breaking point.

Rosie sighed too, fighting back the stinging in her own eyes. She hated to see Maggie upset. She never wanted her daughter to feel as though she couldn't approach her for help, and she certainly didn't want her to ever feel *alone*. But she wasn't about to tell her that this was all okay, either.

"I know it's hard to ask for help sometimes," she said, her tone gentler, "especially when you think you're going to get in trouble for messing up. But you have to remember that Declan and I love you very much, and we will always be here to help you when you need it."

Declan nodded, reaching for Rosie's hand. She took her cue from him and reached for Maggie's as he did the same. Maggie reluctantly let her grown-ups wriggle their fingers beneath the walls of her arm-fortress. Once Rosie felt her smaller hand, she squeezed. Maggie squeezed back, then sniffled.

"I just felt dumb, and like I wasn't a real witch," she admitted, her voice muffled. "But the more I tried to fix it myself, the worse it got. And then it got even *worse* while I was sleeping. And then the next morning they were already everywhere, and it was too late."

"Where are they now?" Rosie asked, leaning down

slightly to try and see Maggie's face through a gap under her armpit.

"Well... most of 'em are in the pen you made," Maggie said, sounding a little hopeful.

"And I'd put money on the rest of them followin' suit quick smart," Declan added with a sly, sideways smile at Rosie. "If Ben doesn't sell his car first."

"So, it's almost fixed," Rosie told Maggie. "We just need to figure out how to get *rid* of them all."

At that, Maggie finally emerged, splotchy-faced and bleary-eyed. "Do you think so?"

Rosie and Declan both nodded.

Maggie sagged a little with relief. "Thanks," she said then. Her arms were crossed over in front of her, but she was still holding their hands. She gave them both a squeeze. "And I'm sorry."

"I'm glad to hear it," Rosie told her, with a sage nod. "I don't like it when you make bad choices, and I *really* don't like it when you lie to us. So as your punishment, you'll be the one responsible for feeding and caring for all the rabbits until we work out how to send them back to wherever it is they came from."

This time, Maggie sagged with a little disappointment. "I was hoping you'd forget the punishment part," she said wistfully.

Rosie quirked a brow, collecting up her cutlery to finish dinner. "Not a chance."

"LORD ABOVE," TAMMY SIGHED ON THE OTHER END OF the phone, sounding more sympathetic with each syllable. "She must've been tryin' to puzzle out how she'd make things right. I hate to think of her all worried like that."

"Don't feel too bad for her," Rosie sassed down the phone. She swung her legs out in front of herself, making the porch swing creak forwards as she enjoyed the cool night air. "She was happy enough to give a comment to a news reporter with a grin on her face and lie to me about it over dinner before coming clean. Caring for the rabbits is a pretty light punishment."

"Are you sure?" Tammy teased. "Ben is still goin' on about the smell of rabbit in in car upholstery. You'd think the thing was a late-model Mustang, not an old Brady Bunch mobile!"

Rosie grinned, imagining Ben with six kids and a perky blonde wife. "I'd settle for the Flintstone's car right about now," she joked, "so a wood-paneled station wagon is just about as flashy as Caesar's chariot in my eyes. Not everyone can afford to buy a BMW with their divorce settlements, you know."

"You're right. But—ugh! I love it so much," Tammy gushed. "if I'd known how wonderful it'd be to have a leather seat huggin' my butt like a broke-in pair of Levis, I woulda kicked Terry out years ago."

Rosie giggled. "Guess it's nice to know he was useful for somethin' in the end!"

"Amen to that," Tammy agreed with a chuckle. But

there was a strange sort of little pause at the end of her laugh, and Rosie didn't know how to continue the joke. She huffed a short breath of her own, her mind falling onto the thing that was most concerning her now that her unruly child was more or less in hand.

Tammy didn't skip another beat. "What's up, sugar?"

"Well," Rosie began. "I hate to say it, but we need to think about what we're gonna do now for our grand opening."

"I know you keep tellin' me you're a witch and not a psychic," Tammy said in an airy voice that couldn't help but lighten the mood, "but if you keep bein' right all the time I'm gonna have to press you for the lottery numbers!"

"Now if I could do that then we would both be driving Beemers," Rosie smiled.

"La-dee-dah!" Tammy laughed.

Rosie tilted her face up to look at the smattering of stars that were visible between cloudy curtains in the sky. "Do you wanna get together this weekend to brainstorm? We could meet at the store. I need to regrow all my stock, and I might be able to help you get any lingering stains out of your lace tablecloths."

"You're a doll," Tammy cooed. "Myles and I are having coffee at the shop on Monday morning—why don't we catch up after that? I made all those bear claws for the Fair, and they're not gonna eat themselves."

"*Now* who's the doll?"

Tammy's blush was almost audible. "I do what I can," she said sweetly. "Until then, behave yourself."

"Yes ma'am," Rosie said, feigning seriousness.

Tammy took the bait. "Don't you ma'am me, ma'am!"

Grinning, Rosie held the phone out in front of her face and prepared to end the call. "Okay. Bye!"

"Bye!"

CHAPTER 4

S unday mornings at Fox Cottage were for yard work. While Rosie wasn't a churchgoer, being out working in nature felt right to her on a day that others counted as a holy day. The added benefit of the warmer weather meant that she had been able to assess the yard for any damage that had cropped up over winter and make gardening plans for the rest of the year.

She was on her knees in the middle of a new garden bed she had dug around the huge oak tree in the middle of the lawn. There was space to eventually lay a path to the grassy base of the tree, where she mentally planned for Declan to install a tree bench ready for the summer. Rosie worked the soil with her trusty old trowel, thoughts of reading under the tree with a tall glass of sweet tea firmly in mind.

Declan was trimming branches from the opposite

side of the tree, perched carefully above the developing garden bed on a ladder. He had one earbud in and was humming tunelessly along to something that sounded like it might have been The Corrs.

Her tummy did a backflip and she smiled to herself at his adorable, terrible tone-deafness. It would have been both jealousy-inducing and a little too much if he had been hot, sweet, good in bed *and* a good singer as well.

She doubled down her efforts, turning the soil in front of her until it was soft, and damp, and rich-looking. The smell of the fresh earth was almost intoxicating and mingled with the scent of geraniums blooming by the porch. Rosie turned her trowel again and again, getting caught in the hypnotic rhythm of her work.

That is, until she saw something shiny that looked like bug legs in the dirt she had just deposited by her right knee. She froze immediately, the spell of her garden ritual rudely snapped like a stray twig. Trowel held in front of her, Rosie scrambled to her feet and then bent forward slightly to poke at the dirt.

Whatever it was *jumped*. It rocketed up into her face, and she felt it scrape against her neck. She threw the trowel, abandoning all hope of a showdown in favor of engaging her flight response. Her hands came up to slap frantically at her neck and cheeks, pausing mid-heartbeat to assess whether the threat remained.

A moment passed. A moment where she couldn't

feel the gross scratching of bug feet on her skin. Then another. Her breathing slowed a little, until a strange pinching sensation directed her attention to her cleavage, where a sizeable cricket seemed to be taking shelter from the human hurricane.

"*Argh!*" Rosie cried, flicking her hands at her boobs as she tried to dislodge the critter without actually having to *touch* it.

Unfortunately, her plan wasn't exactly well thought-out. The cricket only buried itself deeper into the protective crevice between her breasts, making Rosie dance across the garden bed, screaming. She grabbed at her shirt and flapped it madly.

It would have been all over but the therapy at this point, except that Declan, with his excellent powers of observation, had noticed something was amiss down below. He had leaned away from the tree on his ladder to see better, overbalanced on the ladder and then fell backwards.

"*Declan!*"

Rosie started to run towards him, knowing even as she gathered her own magic that she wouldn't be able to react in time to save him.

A strange breeze whipped up, rushing through the space between them like some kind of natural barrier. He simply stopped mid-fall, his hair looking bushy and wild as his head pointed towards the ground and his feet waved up in the air.

Rosie's blood pressure was through the roof. She

could feel her heartbeat thudding in her ears and pulsing like a subwoofer in her chest. The breeze swirled around them again and then swooped away, leading Rosie's gaze to three incredibly *weird* people who had somehow materialized on the lawn several yards in front of her. She grabbed the hem of her t-shirt and yanked it back down to cover her boobs and baby belly. The cricket, unnoticed, hopped away.

The first visitor was a large woman who looked like a corporate secretary. Her mousy brown hair was scraped back from her face into a tight French twist updo. Her eyes were completely black like a shark's and assessed Rosie blankly behind thick-rimmed glasses, as she clutched a clipboard in one hand.

The second was an incredibly tiny, glam-looking drag queen in a long rose-gold ballgown. Her hair was a pixie-cut wig of white feathers, and her lips were painted with a dark brown stain and cinched on one side in contemplation.

The third was a tall man in a simple pair of pants, a white shirt rolled up to his elbows, and suspenders that would have been more fashionable in Victorian London instead of modern Georgia. His dark blonde hair and beard was silvered with age, and both were shaggy in a way that made Rosie wonder about his personal hygiene. His brown boots that looked like they had seen better days were planted in the grass, and a dark green tattoo in the shape of a bramble wound itself around his right forearm and up under the cuff of his shirt.

The only other witches Rosie had ever met were Declan, Gemma, and of course Maggie. She wasn't sure what she would have expected when meeting still more of their kind, but it sure wasn't the circus act that was standing in judgement of her less than five yards away.

With an almost negligent wave of the man's hand, Declan tumbled with reduced momentum to the grass with an *oof*.

"Get up, boy! Ya makin' an ass of yourself!" the man bit out, his thick Irish brogue hardened by his dry, scathing tone as he glanced from Declan to Rosie.

"Hello to you too, Da'," Declan grunted. He rolled into a sitting position, and then got up slowly to dust himself off. His expression was guarded as he looked at the older man, walking over to stand by Rosie.

"Rosie, this is my father—Cillian. Da', meet Rosie."

The man simply inclined his head, as though it would help the insult to roll off his already oily-looking skin.

"Rosemary Bell, I presume?" The woman with the black, dead eyes was fixated on her, one fingertip tapping impatiently on the back of her clipboard.

Rosie lifted her chin defiantly, subconsciously mirroring Declan's father's expression. She hadn't particularly *wanted* to make a bad first impression with Declan's parents, but given that he had just seen her dancing around her lawn half naked with a cricket clinging to her bra she supposed that horse had already bolted.

"You presume correctly," Rosie confirmed with as much bravado as she could muster while holding a t-shirt in front of her, instead of wearing it. She refused to let the heated feeling in her cheeks take hold any more than it already had. Rosie avoided looking directly into the woman's creepy eyes.

Declan shifted his weight beside her, moving closer in what felt like a protective maneuver.

"Excellent," the woman replied without skipping a beat, though her answering smile was too wide and white to be welcoming and did nothing to stop Rosie from thinking of her as a predatory Great White. "We are here to assess the situation, and report back to—"

"Excuse me," Rosie interrupted, "but what situation? And you're here from *where*, exactly?"

The secretary blinked—the first reassuringly human action Rosie had seen her perform—and slowly pressed her free hand to her chest as though to calm herself.

Declan leaned into her ear. "The Council of Witches," he explained in a low voice.

It was Rosie's turn to blink and she frowned, half in confusion and half in amusement. "COW? Seriously?" she asked aloud. He gave her a tiny shake of his head in response, but his warning came too late.

"You," the secretary breathed from behind the smile she was wearing again, "are charged with Negligence of a Magical Minor and endangering the Secrecy of Witches—"

"Wait – what?!" Rosie exclaimed, memories of

having her steps dogged by Sheriff Holt rushing back to her.

"—and you will find, Ms. Bell, that if you keep interrupting me my patience will eventually wear thin and *pop*." The p's in the word 'pop' were accentuated by the woman's dry-looking lips. The queen to her right raised a brow as if to say 'don't act like you weren't warned'.

But Rosie'd had it up to here with being treated like a child. She narrowed her eyes and lifted her chin higher.

"I'm not sure what you're threatening, and I have no idea what the Council of Witches is or what negligence I've committed, but let me be perfectly clear: if you don't start explaining yourself, *my* patience will wear thin and I will physically remove you from my property. Understood?"

The shark-woman's eyebrows rose clear to her hairline.

"Hooboy!" the tiny drag queen crowed with a titter of laughter as she fussed dramatically with one side of her wig. "We got ourselves a live one here, y'all!"

Declan's father was silent, his face unreadable. She didn't think it was a good sign.

The shark-woman was the first to speak. "Please accept the Council's sincere apologies for the intrusion. I am Morgan Blake, High Inquisitor of the Council of Witches."

So the bitch has a name, Rosie thought wryly. She

filed it away mentally, somewhere between 'get the hell off my lawn' and 'fuck you too, Sharknado'. Morgan wafted a hand toward the drag queen and the man in turn. "This is Hella Get-ho, the Council's Mediator, and His Majesty, King Cillian Forrest of the Republic of Ireland, who was invited because of his… close ties to the situation." She glanced at Declan.

"And you're here because you think I'm neglecting my daughter?" Rosie asked pointedly.

Morgan's attention sailed gracefully back to Rosie. "We are here because someone has threatened the Secrecy." She gave a funny little series of blinks, as though the fact should be common knowledge to someone who was magical royalty.

"Look it's like this, girl," the tiny queen said, stepping over the invisible line of authority between the two factions. "The kid created a national news item— and *then* held a damn press conference." She titled her head with a smirk, as though amused by Maggie's audacity. "That shit just ain't *done*."

Morgan cleared her throat.

"What?" The queen tilted her head the other way, planting a hand on one jaunty hip. The sequins on her dress glittered in the late morning sunshine. "We can't just be showin' up on Her Majesty's doorstep like Colonel Klink. She's been Lost her whole damn life— she ain't know the score, *Morgan*."

"Okay," Rosie cut in, because she still ain't know

the score. "So, the 'Secrecy' is the worldwide secret we're all keeping about witches existing?" she asked. She glanced habitually at Declan, who nodded, and then looked back at the Council. "But if the Secrecy is so important, why is this the first time I've heard from—or *of*—the Council? Wouldn't touching base with the heir to a powerful magical line be something of a priority?"

"It would have been," Morgan replied, turning her chin toward Declan, "Had we *known* your magic had come into its own." Declan turned his face away sheepishly, while Cillian crossed his arms and looked the other way. Hella let out a quiet 'mmhmm' of disapproval.

Morgan continued, returning her gaze to Rosie. "How unfortunate for everyone involved."

"Actually," said Rosie with a narrowing of her eyes. "Up until today it was working just fine, and if you had all acted more professionally when you arrived it still would be."

'Morgan' didn't seem too pleased to be called out so brazenly, but Rosie had a pre-teen daughter, so she wasn't particularly impressed or frightened by displeasing rude people. Morgan visibly restrained herself before speaking.

"May we see the child?" she asked, her tone dripping with Splenda.

"The child's *name* is Magnolia," Rosie replied. "She's just tending to the rabbits. If you'll follow me."

A storm was brewing inside of her; a gut-churning tornado that was an uncomfortable mix of shock, dread, and fierce motherly protection. Her gaze slid sideways to Declan again. He reached for her hand, giving it a squeeze while he nodded just once.

"This way."

ROSIE AND DECLAN LED THE COW DOWN THE KITCHEN side of the cottage, around the greenhouse he had built for Rosie in the lead-up to last Christmas. The area was in full bloom now, fit to burst with plants in various stages of growth that Rosie was cultivating for Nourish. Rosie noticed as she returned to the group that the picture-perfect scene seemed to impress Declan's father, who looked over the greenhouse—and the Muscadine grape vine sprawling inside of it—with great interest. His eyes fell to the collection of pots on the nearby potting bench, taking in the little green nubs that were the rabbits' leftovers, before narrowing to slits.

Yikes.

The group rounded the corner into what could be considered the back yard; a smallish clearing that was little more than a patch of grass, some hedges, and the rusted-looking garden shed. As they stepped around the corner, Rosie and Declan ground to a halt. Rosie turned back, searching her mind for a reason to divert the COW back to the front of her cottage. Declan was too busy staring ahead to be of much help. The three other witches stepped around the pair of them with a swish of sequins and authority.

Maggie was standing inside the magical rabbit pen Rosie had created, with one hand held up as though conducting an orchestra. The other hand clasped a bright red apple that was already missing several bites. Her dark brown hair was standing on end as though charged with static electricity, which was perhaps the least surprising thing about the scene.

A score of rabbits floated in mid-air, temporarily disturbing the invisibility spell that was supposed to keep them hidden. An old dustpan, a rake, and a rusted old garbage can moved themselves around the area. The rake and the dustpan occasionally scooped something out of the grass and deposited it into the old garbage can. Handfuls of leafy green lettuce zoomed through the air, ready to reward the floating rabbits for their patience as soon as they were deposited back onto the newly-cleaned ground.

It was like an admittedly less chaotic version of Mickey Mouse's *Fantasia* scene. Despite Maggie breaking the rules and the imminent danger of COW disapproval, Rosie was actually pretty impressed.

"What do ya think you're *doin'?*" Cillian barked, making Maggie jump. With the shock of being discovered, Maggie's arcane energy faltered. The various elements all wobbled mid-air, looking as though they might fall to the ground. One of the rabbits sniffed the wind in anticipation.

Rosie started to gather her energy, focusing on Maggie's magic with the intent to provide a calming forcefield for the spell. But Cillian intervened, just as he had when Declan had been about to fall off his ladder and injure himself. *His* magic was nothing like Rosie's. It was heavy-handed and pushed other energies aside to assert itself instead of seeking to combine and strengthen an existing spell.

"Hey!" Maggie yelped, watching with dismay as her rabbits were zoomed across the pen in straight little lines like an army of fluffy soldiers. Everything else fell to the lawn, as though it had never been enchanted into chores by a ten-year-old in the first place. She looked guiltily at her mom, and then at the three strangers who were obviously *very* annoyed.

"Girl, I *know* you weren't just out here usin' magic all unsupervised," Hella drawled. Maggie looked from Hella to Rosie, and tried to explain.

"I was only cleaning," Maggie protested. "Look how many there are! It'd take me all day to clean otherwise."

"Ya should've thought about *that* before you went an' conjured 'em up in the first place," Cillian muttered darkly, accusation plain in his eyes as he glared at Declan. Rosie took a breath to intervene, but Declan beat her to it.

"Hey," Declan said, throwing a glare of his. "Don't talk to Maggie that way! She's not yours to discipline."

"*Enough!*"

Morgan's roar filled the small area. Everyone immediately fell quiet, turning to look at her in surprise. As soon as she was certain that she had everyone's attention, she lifted her brows and continued talking in a normal tone of voice.

"The Secrecy of our kind is of the utmost importance," she explained archly, "and *all* witches are bound to ensure that the Secrecy is maintained."

Maggie crossed the grass to stand close to her mom, a worried expression on her face. Rosie pursed her lips, wrapping an arm across the top of Maggie's shoulders to pull her closer.

Cillian noticed the exchange, and a soft snort of derision escaped him. "Fact is," he interjected, sounding righteous enough that it made Rosie want to slap him, "you've endangered the Secrecy with ya little *stunt*."

"But I didn't mean to!" Maggie spluttered. "I—"

"You seem to share your mother's inability to wait until someone else has finished speaking," Morgan snapped.

Rosie felt Maggie physically flinch at the harshness of the Inquisitor's words. And then, somewhere deep inside of her, she felt something snap.

"How *dare* you," she said forcefully, setting her shoulders and staring straight into Morgan's dead, black eyes.

"You have come here, to our home," Rosie said, fighting to keep her voice level and poised, "without invitation or warning. You neglected to introduce yourselves, and you have been nothing but rude." She shook her head, her eyes trained on Morgan. "Shame on you all!"

Silence passed over the group again. Maggie had reached up to hold Rosie's arm in support, and Declan was staring at her with open admiration while Hella grinned widely. Cillian's bushy eyebrows had disappeared into the long bangs of his shaggy hair, and Morgan looked as though she was ready to commit a murder... or three.

Maggie might be a pain her ass at times... but what kid *wasn't*? Furthermore, Maggie was *her* pain in the ass, and she would be damned if she was just going to roll over and let three strangers come up in their lives with enough attitude to float the Titanic. Declan had been telling her that she was a Queen for months now. Hella had confirmed it. And now, it was about damn time she started *acting* like it.

Morgan blinked, collecting herself. "Ms. Bell—"

"*Your Majesty*," Rosie corrected her, her tone every bit as harsh as the one Morgan had just used to frighten Maggie.

Hella's expression went from 'Yay, drama!' to 'This is some Jerry Springer brawling level shit' in 0.02 seconds. She lifted her hand to cover her excited grin, her dark plum nail polish shining in the late morning sunshine.

Morgan blanched, pressed her dry, flaky lips together, and then plastered her smile back into place.

"Your... *Majesty*," she said, haltingly and with an unconvincing note of respect. "In addition to protecting the Secrecy, the Council ensures that all witches receive an adequate, if not exemplary, magical education. Rules are to be obeyed, and skills need to be learned. It seems to me that we could kill two birds with one stone by enrolling Magnolia in one of our educational institutions, don't you think?"

Rosie felt ice flow through her veins. Maggie shifted slightly under her hold.

"Educational institutions?" Rosie repeated.

"It means boarding school," Hella said, popping out from where she stood like a bad news whack-a-mole.

"Absolutely not," Rosie declared hotly. "My daughter is staying right here."

"I don't think ya be quite understandin' the situation," Cillian said slowly, his patronizing tone thicker than his accent. "Both of ya have more untapped power than most of the magical community. That means ya *both* need to control ya magic to protect the Secrecy!"

Rosie glared at the leprechaun man. "I'm a bad witch and an unfit mother," she snapped. "Got it."

"No, ya not," Declan said defensively, lifting a hand to her back bracingly.

Rosie shrugged him off, annoyed. "Why didn't you tell me about all this?"

Declan flushed with embarrassment and lowered his voice. "They cast a spell, so they can tell when ya share the Secret." A titter of laughter escaped from Hella, while Cillian rolled his eyes. "At least that's what they tell ya when you're a wee'an," Declan added with a glare at his father. He looked back at Rosie. "I didn't want them knowin' about ya until ya were ready. We were doin' so well on our own. I thought we had it covered."

"Which is all very romantic," Morgan interrupted, and then lifted her eyebrows. "But very stupid." As quickly as Rosie's ire had risen at Declan, it shifted to the person insulting him. But Morgan continued, undaunted. "Magnolia must have a magical education, and from what I can tell, nothing has been put in place to ensure that happens."

Declan stepped back from her slightly, his brows drawn together in concern. Rosie stood a little taller, pulled Maggie a little closer, and looked each of the Council members in the face.

"Thanks for your concern," she said, "but *I'm* what's been put in place to ensure Maggie gets what she needs, and that includes a magical education."

Morgan set her jaw in a hard line.

"If you or Magnolia threaten the Secrecy again, we will have no choice but to declare you as Lost."

"I've been Lost my whole damn life," Rosie said, repeating Hella's earlier proclamation, "And you guys never cared before."

Hella clicked her fingers at Rosie's sass, and then stepped across the divide on the lawn so that she was standing right in front of Rosie.

"Girl, Lost witches are bitches without Council protection," she explained calmly. "That means that no matter what happens—crazy spells out the wah-zoo that go all wrong, disputes between neighborin' realms—you ain't got the Council on your side." She stole a fleeting glance at Maggie. "Also means that a witch can't attend a decent magical school, vote in elections..."

She trailed off slowly, her honey-brown eyes searching Rosie's. Her underlying message was clear. Maggie wouldn't have much of a future if *she* was the heir to Rosie's magical throne.

Almost as though reading Rosie's mind, Morgan spoke up.

"I forget that you know so *little*," she sighed. "There are two types of Lost witches: those who are Lost by banishment, and those who are Lost by circumstance. A witch who merely *happens* to step outside of the Council's sphere of protection—whatever their reasoning—is Lost by circumstance. They are able to submit to rejoin the Council. But to be *declared* Lost is to be banished from the Council forever."

Morgan looked entirely unimpressed that Rosie didn't understand this basic concept, but Rosie just lifted her chin. "I see."

"Banishment is the most severe punishment the Council doles out," Cillian added. His eyes burned into

Rosie's face, and she was outraged as she felt as though he was giving her a silent warning. "There's no goin' back."

Her gaze bore back into Cillian. "My daughter isn't leaving my side." She looked at each of the COW representatives in turn. "Not for you, not for anyone. Powerful or not, I want to be treated just like anyone else, and be left to raise my daughter on my own terms."

Morgan tilted her chin. "Very well. If you can prove that you can competently teach your daughter the magical skills and information that she will need to grow into a capable and responsible witch, then you may educate her at home and still remain under the Council's jurisdiction."

Rosie let her shoulders relax. "*Thank* you," she said, but Morgan continued before she could say anything else.

"We will return to complete an audit of Magnolia's magical ability on her eleventh birthday."

Rosie froze. Maggie gasped, "But that's only two weeks away!"

"Is it?" Morgan asked, glancing from Maggie to Rosie. "Well, you did want to be treated like everyone else." She turned her back on them both and began to walk from the rabbit pen. "Good luck."

Hella gave Rosie a sympathetic smile, and then leaned down so that she was face to face with Maggie. "You be good for your Mama now, baby-girl."

Maggie nodded mutely.

"And for Hecate's sake," she said, side-eyeing Declan, "give your woman a damn run-down."

Rosie turned her attention to Declan briefly as the only person left towards whom she might direct her anger. She didn't know that she truly blamed him, so the only thing she could think behind the mask of her glare was, *'Yeah! What she said!'*

CHAPTER 5

Declan's attention turned to his father as Morgan and Hella began to leave.

"What the *fuck*, Da'?"

Cillian quirked a bushy brow, his face stern. "I could ask ya the same!"

The response was loaded, and Declan stalked towards his father.

Rosie leaned forwards. "Maggie," she said softly. "Please go to your room. I'll be along soon."

As Maggie sighed—no doubt disappointed to miss out on the adult drama—and made for the house, Rosie walked over to Declan and his father. Declan's face was as red as his hair.

"What do you think you're doin', rockin' up here with the damn *Inquisitor* to try and take Maggie away?!"

"Don't be gettin' ya knickers in a knot, now," Cillian blustered. "Ya always go off half-cocked an' end up gettin' the wrong end of the stick!"

"How else should I be reactin'?" Declan fired back, his accent sounding almost as thick as his dad's in the heat of the moment.

"Ya should've been tellin' the Council what ya knew about all this from the start!" Cillian glanced behind his son at Rosie and hesitated as though he didn't want to discuss any of this in front of her. "I think this is a family matter, Declan."

"Rosie *is* my family. Anythin' you have to say, ya can say in front of her."

"*She* is ya family?" Cillian sputtered. "This woman," he jutted his chin towards Rosie, "has no control over her own magic, no control over her child's magic, and is dangerously close to removin' herself from Council association!" He sniffed. "What kind of match is that for my son?"

"Luckily for me," Declan shot back, just as Rosie's was about to tell his dad where to go, "I don't need your approval when it comes to my choice in partners."

"You've demonstrated that well enough," his dad snorted, before glancing slyly at Rosie. "Or does she not know about your little jaunt in bloody Las Vegas?"

Declan shook his head slightly. "Rosie knows everything. You're gonna have to try harder than that, Da'."

Cillian did seem genuinely surprised to find out that

Rosie and Declan were much closer than he'd thought. "I just want what's best for you, that's all. What if this woman and her daughter get banished, what then?"

"Is that what this is about, Da'?" Declan scoffed with mirthless laughter. "Or is there some political reason behind all this, like always?"

Cillian threw his hands up in the air. "Ah—you're stubborn, just like ya Ma."

"Don't bring Ma into this! You're the one who was here with the Mod Squad. So, tell me why." Declan folded his arms, glaring expectantly at his father.

"The Council is tryin' to do the right thing here," Cillian said, forcing his tone into something a touch more civil, "Uncontrolled magic is dangerous, and endangerin' the Secrecy is even worse. Just look at all the innocents who died the last time the Secret got out." Cillian shifted tactics. "The girl will get a grand education at an Irish school. I'll see to it."

Declan's face fell as he recognized what his father was saying. "Oh, so that's it? Rosie's too much of a liability and Declan's disappointed ya again, so you'd better get Maggie under ya control, then?"

Cillian clamped his mouth shut, his face blank.

Declan barked a harsh laugh. "Nice one, Da'. Just when I thought things might *actually* improve between us, ya have to go an' prove me wrong."

"Declan, I—" Cillian began, but his son cut him down.

"Get the *fuck* out of here," Declan growled. "And

don't come back. Don't call me, don't try to get me to come 'round. I'm done with you and ya games, and I don't give a shit about the damned Prophecy."

The color drained out of Cillian's face, and with his scruffy hair and old-timey clothes he suddenly seemed like an old man. He stared into his son's eyes for a long moment, then looked at Rosie appraisingly. Then he nodded, just once, and left.

Declan turned to her, breathing hard after the altercation with his father.

"Rosie, I—"

"Declan!" Rosie interrupted, placing her hands on Declan's biceps. "You just cut yourself off from your Dad! Are you alright? Are you sure?" Rosie's gaze darted between Declan's eyes, and he relaxed into her arms, putting his hands on her elbows.

"Ah, that's..." he started, and then looked Rosie directly in the eyes. "We cut each other off about once a decade." He shrugged. "'Sides, he deserved it."

Rosie felt her chest swell at the idea of Declan being so devoted to her, even if he could be a bit of a putz. He lifted his hands from her elbows to her cheeks and looked into her face.

"But how are *you* doin', love?" He shook his head and Rosie blinked when his nice, soothing touch suddenly vanished from her cheeks so that he could gesture nervously. "This is a lot. Like, I *know* it's a lot. And we've had so much else going on—first Randy, then Gemma, then Holt. All while trying to settle into a groove together and keep everything ticking. I didn't think any of this stuff was as important as what we had goin' on at the time, I guess."

His hands enveloped hers, warm and steady in the moment. "I'm sorry Rosie. I didn't think that they would come down on us like this. They rarely interfere—"

Rosie scoffed. "Yeah. I got that. They made an exception for little ol' me."

Declan snorted. "If ya were *little old you*, they wouldn't be interferin'." He raised a hand to push a lock of hair out of her face. "Ya magic's crazy. So is Maggie's."

Holding back a sigh, she leaned forward to plant the top of her forehead into Declan's chest. "And now I have fourteen days to show Maggie everything she needs to know, or else they're gonna take her." Ever since the Council had shown up, Rosie's emotions had been expanding inside of her. She tried to blink away the feeling of tears beginning to well in her eyes. "And the worst part about it all, is that your dad's right! How can I teach her magic when I'm still learning it myself? How can I protect her from growing up like I did, without her family by her side?"

Declan folded her into a hug, nestling his cheek against the top of her head. "*We* have fourteen days to teach Maggie," he corrected her sweetly, "and no matter what happens, Maggie'll always have us by her side. This isn't a case of history repeatin', love."

Rosie closed her eyes, praying to anyone with god-like status who might happen to be listening in. "How can you possibly know that?"

"Because no matter what happens," he told her, "the three of us will face it together."

AFTER A LITTLE TIME SPENT ON THE FRINGES OF THE woods, Rosie felt like her head was clear enough to go talk with her daughter. She knocked gently on the plain knotted pine door to Maggie's bedroom: a magical little realm where her big imagination had run free since they had arrived nearly a year ago.

Maggie's voice was muffled behind the door. "Come in."

Rosie opened the door, her eyes adjusting to the late afternoon shadows that played over what she had come to think of as Maggie's 'collection'. The round porthole window that Maggie adored was right next to the bed, looking out on a thick section of Needlepoint Woods like a watchful eye. The shelf above the bed held various artefacts that Maggie had found in the woods themselves; pine cones, a rusted thimble, bird feathers, and odd-shaped stones.

The tank that her dad had occupied in turtle form sat on the second-hand desk, which now held his empty turtle shell. Her school books and some scattered markers occupied the rest. Maggie was under her bed, her top half hidden by the purple patchwork quilt that Tammy had bought her for Christmas from the Church craft sale.

Rosie closed the door softly, pausing to look at the beautiful picture taped to the back of it—her, Declan, Tammy, and Maggie, all together. Even Randy made an appearance, still in turtle form, sitting on top of Maggie's head. Smiling, Rosie took a seat on the edge of the bed.

"Whatcha doin'?" she asked, kicking off her shoes so that she could sit cross-legged.

"Reading," Maggie replied. She held her book out from under the edge of the quilt, so that Rosie could see the cover.

"Anne of Green Gables," Rosie read aloud, nodding. "Solid choice."

"Thanks," Maggie said, falling silent for a moment. Then she crawled out from beneath the bed, putting her torch and book on her desk before sitting next to her mom on the bed. "Were those people really from the Council of Witches?"

Rosie's face felt like it was made of stone. "Yeah Pumpkin, they were."

"They didn't seem very nice," Maggie observed, threading her fingers together, "apart from the one in the sparkly dress."

"I guess it's because they had to come here to tell us bad news." Rosie shrugged lightly. "It's a little difficult to have a good time when you know people aren't gonna like what you have to say to them."

Maggie unthreaded her fingers before threading them again. "I'm sorry I was using magic to clean out the rabbit poop," she said quietly.

Rosie's heart squeezed with love for the tiny human she was doing her best to raise. Being a mom wasn't easy, Lord knew. But she remembered being a kid and that hopeless kind of feeling that came along with trying to find her place in a world that was constantly changing around her. The COW's threat had made her even more terrified of something happening to prevent her from being able to give Maggie more stability than she'd had.

But on the other hand, if Maggie didn't learn now that there were rules and expectations in life, it would be a harder lesson later. How much slack could she cut her daughter on account of dads who became turtles, or evil witches, or crazy Sheriffs, or starting a new school? There was always going to be any number of excuses without Rosie serving them up for her.

"Are you?" she asked at last, striving to keep her tone light. "I kinda feel like you're only sorry that you got *caught.*"

Maggie realized that her apology wasn't going to earn her a Get Out of Jail Free card, and sagged a little. "I just want to be able to use my powers to make my life easier," she admitted, trying to mimic Rosie's tone even though there was more raw emotion in hers. "What's the point of even being a witch if I'm never allowed to do magic?"

"But in order to be allowed to do magic you have to prove that you can do it responsibly," Rosie told her, "not by just continuing to do it whenever you feel like it. And especially not by doing it behind my back!"

Maggie sighed, "There's no point even talking about this. You're never going to change your mind!"

Rosie pursed her lips. "About letting you loose, unsupervised, with powerful magic? You're right, I won't."

"You just don't listen to me." Maggie flopped back onto her bed, staring up at the ceiling. Rosie couldn't help but think that if her daughter was this dramatic at ten, she was in for a helluva time when puberty kicked in for real.

"*You* don't listen to *me*," Rosie insisted. "You think you can do anything you want, whenever you want, and you don't stop to think about the consequences or how it might affect other people."

Maggie didn't respond, other than to roll over on her side so that she was facing the wall. Rosie watched her for a few seconds, her heart feeling a little worse for wear. A niggling voice in the back of her mind wanted to know how she was going to teach her kid the right ways to use her magic, when she wasn't even sure on how to do that herself.

After a minute or so, Rosie let herself out, closing Maggie's bedroom door behind her.

IF THE COW SHOWING UP AT FOX COTTAGE HAD BEEN akin to a live hand grenade being dropped right in the middle of their lives, then the next day was filled with the tension of waiting for it to explode. Every conversation with Maggie was strained and awkward. No matter how many different ways Rosie tried to find a way to express the grown-up side of things, Maggie just wasn't picking up what she was putting down.

It felt like the whole house was holding its breath.

Rosie was busy sorting laundry in the bathroom, keeping an ear out for Maggie who was cleaning her room while Declan tidied the rest of the house. Having her very own washing machine—courtesy of her wonderful friends—was a blessing. The long pilgrimage to the Kwik Kleen in town had been the bane of her existence during their early days in Mosswood.

She bent to stuff Maggie's school clothes, Declan's work clothes, and her Go-Go Mart polo shirts into the machine, swinging back to grab an armful of towels for good measure. By the time she had turned back to the machine, the first bunch of laundry had been pitched out onto the floor. Rosie straightened with a huff, just as the machine coughed up a sock, sending it flying towards the already discarded pile of clothes.

"Don't start with me," she warned the machine as she raised a brow, her free hand perching on her hip with attitude. "We still have *hours* before I can drink wine in good conscience."

Just went to show that you could take the machine out of the Kwik Kleen, but you might *never* get the Kwik Kleen out of the *machine.*

She shoved the bundle of towels into the machine, held them down for a moment, and then kept one eye on the machine as she retrieved the clothes from the bathroom floor.

Nothing happened.

"That's what I thought," she said triumphantly, closing the lid of the machine before adding her detergent and turning it on.

She sighed. All of her chores were done, and Declan was still doing his. Letting things sit with Maggie was only playing into the jitters she felt in her bones. It was time to take action, and she knew just the right place to blow off some steam.

Maggie was surprised when Rosie stuck her head into the bedroom.

"Everything okay, Mom?"

"Yep," Rosie said, glancing around the mostly-tidy room. "You about done?"

"Yep," Maggie nodded.

"Close enough. Come with me."

Maggie bit her lip, hesitating. "Am I in trouble again?"

Rosie felt a familiar surge of mom-guilt spike in her

stomach. "No, honey," she said. "We're just taking a field trip is all."

"A field trip?" Maggie rushed to pull on her sneakers.

Declan had just finished putting away the clean dishes when he was led from the kitchen by both hands —one in Rosie's, the other in Maggie's.

The three of them left the cottage, breathing the fresh air deeply as they crossed the front lawn and took one of Rosie's well-worn forest paths. They were all quiet, enjoying the embrace of the woods as they trekked. It wasn't long until they reached their destination.

The field was full of the promise of early summer. The grass had grown since last year, and bees hummed happily from one tiny yellow meadow flower to the next. It would have been a wonderful day for a picnic, if it hadn't been for the fact that the three of them were there to work.

"What are we doing here?" Maggie asked suspiciously.

"You see that fallen log in the middle of the field?" Rosie asked, pointing to a gap in the grass about a hundred yards from where they were standing.

Maggie squinted. "... yeah?"

"You're gonna roll it all the way to the edge of the woods," Rosie grinned "With your magic."

Declan glanced at Rosie, cocking an eyebrow.

It was as though someone had thrown a bucket of excitement over Maggie's head. "Really?"

Rosie nodded slowly. "Really." Then she turned to Declan. "Can you help us?"

"Of course." His eyes sparkled with amusement and turned to Maggie. "First," he said calmly, "You want to try and quiet your mind. You need to be as free from distraction as you can possibly be. Okay?"

"Okay," Maggie said, instinctively closing her eyes. Rosie and Declan smiled at each other, bolstered by having an eager student.

"Take a deep breath in," Rosie said, trying to sound gentle and hypnotic, "and then let it out. In again... and out. Good. Let your mind feel light and airy, almost as though it's being blown through the field like a dandelion puff."

Declan nodded his approval of Rosie's description. "Now that you're relaxed, start to gather in your magic. But don't let it out," he warned. "You need to hold it inside of you."

Maggie pressed her lips together, but it wasn't long before the tip of her tongue snuck out, her eyebrows askew with concentrated effort. Rosie's smile widened.

"Now it's gonna want to wriggle and jump out of your hands, a bit like a playful puppy," Rosie said, earning her an emphatic nod from Maggie who looked like she was struggling with the effort of keeping her grip. "You wanna hold it tightly enough to stop it from getting away, but not so tightly that you hurt it."

"Okay," Maggie grunted.

"Got it?" Declan asked her. She nodded.

"Right. Slowly lift up ya hand towards the direction of the log, and let ya magic just begin to slip through your fingers—a bit like how it feels when you let sand slip through them at the beach."

The sound of wood cracking and shifting sounded in the middle of the field.

"I'm doing it!" Maggie cried excitedly, her eyes flying open.

A loud 'pop' filled the air. Declan and Rosie both looked up in time to see the log fling up into the air before doing a somersault and land several yards away from where it had been. Rosie couldn't help but think that it looked like a one of those Scottish log tossing games.

"Oops! I'm sorry!" Maggie quickly apologized.

"It's okay," Rosie soothed, one hand outstretched. "That's why we came out here into the woods where we can't do too much damage. Come on," she said, "we'll get a bit closer."

They started off across the field, the long, sweet grass swishing around their knees like a strange green lake as they went. Butterflies danced here and there, and soft birdsong floated down from the trees.

"I wish we could pick up our house and put it in the middle of this field," Maggie said suddenly. "It's so beautiful here."

"It *is* beautiful here," Rosie agreed, squinting as she glanced around. "But we couldn't do that."

Maggie seemed surprised. "Why not? You could just use magic to do it."

"Well, I don't think the field would look as pretty as it does if we had our quirky little house right in the middle of it. Do you?"

"I guess not," Maggie conceded thoughtfully.

"And then there's the fact that this place is powerfully magical all on its own."

"You mean because of Gemma?"

Rosie and Declan shared a brief look. "No hon," Rosie said, resting a hand on Maggie's shoulder as they neared the up-ended log. "Because *our* magic has been poured into this place, for multiple reasons. Every time you do magic, you leave a little bit of yourself behind."

"Oh," Maggie glanced at the log. "I never really thought about it that way."

Rosie nodded sagely. "Just because you *can* use magic, doesn't mean you always *should*,"

"Uh-huh," Declan agreed. "That's why you need to listen to your Mum and only practice magic when one of us is around to help you. One day you'll be able to do it all on your own, but for right now it's just safer this way."

Maggie groaned a little. "You sound like 'Sesame Street for Witches'," she complained. Rosie glanced at Declan, who flattened his lips together.

"One, ah-ah-ah!" he mimicked the Count, and

Maggie giggled despite how Very Grown Up she was. Rosie smiled though her heart ached. Why couldn't her child just stay adorable and little forever?

"Now. Let's try again," Declan said with a crooked grin, leaving Rosie with her unspoken, impossible wishes.

CHAPTER 6

"This is absolute heaven," Rosie sighed around a mouthful of bear claw, relaxing on the beat-up old armchair that Tammy had sewn a cheerful new yellow cover for. "Exactly what I needed. *Thank you.*"

The transformation that had come over the tiny space that once housed *Oh, Shoot* was incredible. Previously stuffed full of camouflage masculinity, Tammy and Rosie had cleaned the building from top to bottom and white-washed all the unsealed wood. The end result was a pleasing mixture of white wood and exposed brick, none of which smelled like any kind of animal urine.

Tammy had poured the profits from the sale of the hunting merchandise back into the store, buying gorgeous celestial-inspired light fittings, and having a long white counter installed right along one of the walls. They had repurposed what furniture they could, bought a huge, brightly patterned rug, and filled the rest of the space with an assortment of second-hand couches, tables, and chairs. The windows along the front of the store had been deep-cleaned before Rosie created living curtains for them with an assortment of creeping vines.

"You're so welcome," Tammy said, curled up on the couch across from Rosie. "After the way everythin' panned out over the last few days, I felt a little sugar was mandatory."

"You got that right," Rosie smiled wryly, leaning forward as far as she dared to clunk her takeout coffee cup against Tammy's in cheers.

"I saw a story on Channel 4 News that said the crazy influx of white rabbits in Mosswood had all escaped through a broken fence at a nearby rabbit farm," Tammy told her, peering over the rim of her cup. "Maybe you could put those magical publicity powers to good use advertising the launch of Nourish."

Rosie blinked. "I didn't use magic to make any news cover-ups," she said, making Tammy raise her brows.

"Well if it wasn't *you*," her friend asked, "then who was it?"

A cold chill settled over Rosie's shoulders and she pressed her lips together with a sigh. "I'll bet it was the damn COW," she sighed.

Tammy tilted her head. "What cow?"

Rosie gave Tammy the run-down, ending with as dramatic a re-telling of the COW's visit as she had the energy for.

"Well at least that's helpful," Tammy pointed out. "In a way?"

"Yeah," Rosie agreed begrudgingly. "But at what cost?"

Tammy shifted back into her seat. "I can't imagine what a shock it must have been to have them show up on your doorstep!"

"Well, it sure wasn't a picnic." Understatement of the year. Rosie was haunted by the blank depth of Morgan's inky eyes, but her bigger worry was the real possibility of losing Maggie to an honest-to-goodness Hogwarts. "And it's not like they were even helpful? They came, they delivered their little ultimatum, they left." She sipped her coffee, hastily swallowing it to add, "—and Declan's father was a total dick!"

Tammy pulled a face. "Ugh, I'm sorry. I know the struggles of havin' in-laws that ain't worth the breath you spend on 'em."

"I guess it doesn't matter too much," Rosie lied. She grabbed her notebook and pen from the arm of the chair, and unofficially started their brainstorming session by writing 'Nourish' in the middle of the page before drawing a thought-cloud around it. "Declan wasn't impressed with him—they obviously aren't close. Even less so now, since he basically ran his dad out of town."

"If that means anything," Tammy remarked sadly. "Sleeping dogs never stay sleepin'. Sooner or later they've just gotta get up and bark at someone." She paused, pursing her lips. "And what are you gonna do about Maggie?"

Wasn't that the million-dollar question?

Rosie shrugged, scared that if she let on just *how* worried she was about what they would do about Maggie, she would end up a blubbering heap. "We started showing her some basic stuff," she said instead. "She's pretty good, too... when she can concentrate long enough to finish a task. But I just don't know if we're gonna be able to get her ready in time."

And there it was. The tiny, unmistakable quaver of tears worming their way into the end of her sentence.

Tammy didn't miss a trick. "Awww hon," she cooed, hopping up from the couch to come and perch on the arm of Rosie's chair. She rubbed her friend's back soothingly. "I'm sure you'll think of somethin'! Where there's a will, there's a way—and you're the strongest willed person I know!"

Rosie managed a weak smile, before she swiped the beginnings of her tears away. "I appreciate the faith you have in me. But I don't know. It's like the Council *wants* her to fail— or at least Morgan does. They want Maggie in one of their schools, where they can make her into whatever they want her to be."

"Well, it's our job to make sure that doesn't happen," Tammy said stubbornly.

Rosie half-shrugged and took an enormous bite of her bear claw. "Goff any ideash?"

"I have some ideas for your table manners," Tammy admonished, making Rosie smile a little even if she didn't want to. "And maybe? I've been teachin' Sunday School for a long time now. But when I was just startin' out, I didn't have a clue what to teach those kids. I knew my scripture, and I knew what I wanted the lesson themes to be. But I had to find ways to make Bible study *fun* for kids, who don't typically have huge attention spans at the best of times, let alone when they're learning about the 'boring' Bible." Tammy whispered the word 'boring' and emphasized it with air-quotes, so the Lord wouldn't make the mistake of thinking that *she* could ever class the Good Book as anything less than riveting entertainment.

"That sounds like Maggie alright," Rosie agreed. "What did you do?"

Tammy flipped her hair dramatically, a smug expression commandeering her girlish features. "Googled it," she smirked.

Whatever Rosie had been expecting Tammy to say, it's hadn't been *that*. It took her a moment to register that her friend was serious, and somehow that was even funnier than if Tammy had been actively trying to crack a joke. A laugh bubbled up out of Rosie, followed by another. A third, and it could be considered in some circles that she'd just managed to *chuckle*.

"You can laugh," Tammy sassed her, unphased. "I

found a whole bunch of lesson plans, and printables, and other stuff all over the internet. Some I combined, some I discarded, and some I outright claimed for my classroom. I made them all into a big pink lesson-plan folder that sits on my desk in the Sunday School room to this day."

Rosie grinned cheekily, scribbling 'offer weekly craft classes' on her brainstorming page. "I don't really think that there will be magical lesson plans on the internet," she pointed out, "but I love the idea of making my own lesson book!"

Tammy nodded encouragingly, pleased that she had been able to get a smile out of Rosie even though the situation was dire. "I think you'll be surprised at what you can find on the world wide web these days," she added, sounding less tech-savvy the more she used terms like 'world wide web'. "But it's up to you! I really don't know what other things you could try. Maybe Declan could tutor her?"

Rosie smirked, "Declan's attention span is possibly worse than Maggie's."

It was Tammy's turn to laugh. She covered her mouth shyly, as though feeling guilty for making fun of Declan, before she shook her head. "Well, maybe that's an unexpected bonus. Some kids learn better when they have a class buddy!"

"I'll keep that in mind," Rosie said, thinking she was more likely to strangle Declan than want to have to teach *two* people magic she didn't know the half of.

Tammy sipped her coffee, smiled, and nodded at Rosie's notes. "What do you think we should do for this launch, then?"

Rosie held back a sigh. "I know you're dying to get going," she said, "so I just wanna say that I understand completely if your answer to my next question is yes. But would you mind terribly if we postpone the launch until after Maggie's audit? I really don't know how I will concentrate on anything else right now, and I still have shifts at the Go-Go to cover."

"Of *course* I don't mind," Tammy said immediately, pouring her sympathy into her tone. "I understand. Besides, it will mean that we have extra planning time. What have you written down about craft classes?" she added, peering over at Rosie's page.

ROSIE WAS GLAD THAT THE GO-GO MART WAS ONE thing in her life that never changed. The same layout, the same customers buying the same items, the same cheerful boss. Though she would rather be working in her own store, her current shifts with Ben were a source of great comfort to her. The first half of the afternoon had gone without a hitch, time passing in a flurry of stocking shelves and unpacking produce. By the time her break came around, her feet were ready for a rest.

She flopped into the armchair on the loading dock of the Go-Go, having traded her chair at Nourish for this one only temporarily. She cracked open her can of Coke and reached for her phone. Before she even realized what she was doing, Rosie had opened her internet browser and typed in 'learn magic in Georgia'.

And then she nearly dropped it, when her search returned twelves pages of results. She would have to admit to Tammy that she'd been right—apparently pagans could use the internet to build their education, too!

Rosie scrolled through the listings, until she noticed one in particular.

Sanctuaire Sacré —your one-stop-shop for all your magical, wiccan, and pagan shopping requirements...

An actual *magic store?* A thrilled of excitement electrified her veins, and Rosie suddenly felt invigorated. She clicked the link and was immediately transported to an inky-blue website, decorated with golden constellations. With a quirked brow, she navigated to find the shop's address and opening hours.

Open Monday—Friday.
1020 Bull Street, Savannah, Georgia.

It was already Thursday, and Savannah was a six-hour drive away.

But the wheels in Rosie's head were already turning,

and she swiped out of the website to open up a text message to Declan instead.

Fancy a road trip tomorrow?

His reply came back almost instantly.

I'll go to the ends of the earth with you, my Queen. Where are you taking me?

With a grin, her next text was to Tammy.

Sorry for the short notice, but the internet gave me a lead on lesson planning for Maggie. Can you keep her for me tomorrow night?

Of course I can, Tammy texted back. Then another message came through.

Told ya!

While Rosie didn't hold out a lot of hope that they would find exactly what they needed in Savannah, options were options. It felt good to do something proactive in her mission to teach Maggie the ways of magic.

THEIR ROAD TRIP BEGAN THE NEXT DAY AFTER THEY HAD dropped Maggie at school, and left her overnight stuff with Tammy. It was the second time Rosie had left Maggie with her dear friend, and judging by the excitement on Maggie's face, Rosie and Declan were sure to come home to fun stories about staying up too late and making candy.

The standard highway landscape slipped past the windows of the truck, Rosie's head resting back and her hand looped absently through Declan's as he drove. There was a hum of music from the radio, but it was too soft for her to be able to make out the song. It suited her just fine—her brain was full of thoughts, anyway.

What if they didn't find anything useful? What if Maggie wasn't able to learn enough in time—and what exactly would she be tested *on?* Rules, probably, but what rules? How could they prepare her for something so obtuse?

As though sensing her thoughts, Declan began to draw slow, lazy circles on the back of her hand with his fingertip. It pulled her back to the moment, and Rosie was grateful. Above all, she needed to focus right now and not fall into a cavernous pit of anxiety.

"I booked a room for us in this little motel just out of town for the night," she told him. "It's nothin' fancy, but it'll give us time to rest and come up with a game plan on the drive home tomorrow."

"A night with the hottest woman on earth?" He

glanced at her, his crooked grin coming into play. "Feels like I've won the lottery."

Rosie smiled, tugging his hand closer to her body as she reached to turn the radio up slightly. "I'm pretty sure the room has one of those vibrating beds."

"Bloody hell," Declan laughed, shaking his head as he tried to concentrate on the road.

CHAPTER 7

D riving into Savannah felt like floating into a dream. The leafy streets were well-proportioned and felt intimate, with a history smothering everything like sweet soft butter on fresh biscuits. The cars and people were modern enough, but the architecture was so stately and full of Southern grace that Rosie decided that if she ever left Mosswood, Savannah would be the place for her in a heartbeat.

They drove slowly along Bull Street, their eyes peeled for *Sanctuaire Sacré*. Making their way towards the store made Rosie feel nervous for some strange reason. Easily running half the length of the ground floor of a squat double-storied building, the store front was painted the same deep blue that had featured on their website.

Large plate-glass windows better suited to a clothing store bore hand-lettered advertisements; crystal balls—

tarot readings—incense—candles. The brass door handle was oval-shaped, with a large star carved into it. Rosie found herself glancing over her shoulder as they walked down the sidewalk, relief surrounding her like a warm hug as soon as the door had closed behind them.

"Wow," Declan said under his breath as the pair of them stopped to look around.

It was Terry's hunting store all over again, except with better-looking (and better-smelling) stock. Dimmed lighting from numerous jewel-toned lanterns bathed the cavernous room with a soothing atmosphere, and Rosie could smell the scent of fresh lemons mixed with frankincense and jasmine.

"You can say that again," she murmured back.

As her eyes adjusted to their darker surroundings, she could see a wealth of things in their immediate vicinity. A small round table was stacked high with what appeared to be different cast-iron cauldrons in various sizes. A tiered stand behind it overflowed with various crystals, glinting prettily in the light.

Declan turned to peer along the pathway further into the shop and was hit in the face by a small witch on a broomstick that was suspended from the ceiling. "Bloody hazard," he grunted, lifting a hand to brush an assortment of hanging fairies and pegasi out of his way. Rosie only half heard him, because her attention had been captured by a huge, tortoiseshell Maine Coon cat who was laying majestically on a silver cushion by the window.

"Oh, *hello*," she breathed, "Aren't you just *gorgeous*?"

The cat inclined its head, looking at her with incredible golden eyes before it blinked slowly.

"And he knows it," said a voice with a light French accent off to her right.

A man in his late forties or early fifties smiled at her, setting off the wrinkles around his hazel eyes. His hair was dark brown, with silver at the temples.

Rosie smiled back, holding her hand out for the cat to sniff. "Why be modest when you can be a star."

"Oh, you two will get along famously," the man agreed with a smile. "I'm Francois, and that's Fabien. He likes you," Francois nodded, seeming pleased.

Declan had doubled back to join the conversation, the expression on his face wary as he eyeballed the rather large cat. Suddenly, his nose twitched and he pulled a strange face, screwing up his eyes and clapping his hands over his nose and mouth. "Ahh-*choo!*"

"You not so much," Francois announced dryly.

"Feelin's mutual," Declan added with a sniff.

"Not everyone understands the allure of cats," Francois shrugged, speaking to Rosie as though they were already old friends. "Magnificent creatures, and highly intelligent." He turned to walk deeper into the store, motioning for them to follow. "What can I do for you good folk?"

Rosie took a deep breath. It was hard not to feel overwhelmed by all the things that surrounded them, and aside from a quick glance back at Fabien, who swished his tail and watched her calmly, she didn't know where to look first.

"I'm not even sure you'll be able to help us," she admitted, "but do you have anything for… learning magic?"

Francois took Rosie in more fully, and Rosie got the distinct impression they were both trying to decide how much to say to each other. "*Mais oui,*" he finally replied. "That is what we do." He trotted off with purpose, twitching two fingers over his shoulder to beckon them to follow. "And who is doing the learning?"

"My daughter," Rosie admitted after a brief hesitation. "She's turning eleven."

Francois paused before a bookcase overflowing with both modern and older leather-bound books, but at hearing the age of the student he spun on his heel and continued walking. Rosie almost laughed.

While Francois was leading them through the store, twisting and turning with practiced ease around his many displays, Fabien the Cat had risen from his perch and followed along the top of a counter running the length of the room. He paused where Rosie was still staring at the books and stood on his haunches to bat at a rope that dangled from a fringed valance atop the bookcase. Rosie reached to pull the rope away, but the cat beat her to the punch by sinking his claws into the knot at the end of the rope and leaping from the counter.

He swung down, pulling the valance rope with him, and the bookcase behind it gave a great shudder.

"Fabien!" Francois chided as he rushed back toward them, eyes wide. Rosie took a step back just in time to avoid the bookcase as it swung toward her. Francois put himself between her and the open room the bookcase revealed, spreading his arms to create a barrier. "You don't want to see the stockroom," he said with a tight laugh.

But before he could shut the door back, a warm light began to glow through the opening. He spun in surprise. Behind him, lanterns had just breathed into life to illuminate the room beyond.

"Or... maybe you do," he said slowly.

Behind the shopkeeper were tables and shelves full of various crystal balls, books, tarot cards, quills, crystals, and a variety of other vaguely witchy things. Fabien leaped up onto one of the tables as though to hold court over the objects. Francois turned to glare at him.

"You could have just said so," he said. Fabien meowed in reply.

Rosie was too taken with the magical assortment to notice their spat much. Francois addressed his next remark to his human companions.

"*This* is our assortment of magical aids."

Declan slipped a supportive arm around Rosie, peering at the various items on the table with interest.

"What would you recommend?" she asked, taking a long, deliberate breath and refocusing.

"Oh, that's between the witch and her tool," Francois said, as though he dared not even suggest anything. His attention was diverted by the sound of the door at the front of the shop opening. He glanced in that direction. "Have a little browse—I'll be back with you in just a moment."

"Thank you," Rosie said, as he went to tend his new customers.

Declan squeezed so tightly past Rosie that she was almost unbalanced. She turned to give him a look, but his eyes were glued to the cat.

"I think that's a familiar," he said in a whisper.

Rosie glanced back at the feline when his words belatedly registered. She whispered back. "Like... a witch's familiar? That's a thing?"

"Kind've," Declan agreed with a shrug. "But they're humans, not animals. They can become animals when they're bound to a witch, you know, so they can serve the witch without being suspected. But they start as humans." He placed a hand on either of Rosie's shoulders as he stepped further behind her, as though she could shield him from allergens and creepy magic alike. "The magic you used to turn Randy into a turtle was a kind of familiar magic," he explained, "Just, not finished."

Rosie eyed the cat more suspiciously now. "What does the human get out of it?" It was no wonder witches got such a bad rap, if they just went around enslaving people.

"Whatever their heart desires, usually," Declan shrugged, "within reason. It's usually a fair trade."

Rosie lifted an eyebrow at Fabien, who yawned at Declan's apparent fear. "Then I'm not sure it's any of our business," she said.

"Right," Declan agreed, while keeping Rosie between him and the cat, anyway. She picked up a small leather-bound book and flipped idly through the pages.

"I don't think that's gonna help," he shook his head. "It's blank.

"Nope," Rosie sighed, putting down the book as she waited for something else on the table to take her fancy.

Declan held up a battered, ancient-looking ouija board box.

"Oh, *Hell* no," Rosie declared, slapping his hand to make him put it down.

"Yeah fair enough," Declan agreed, putting the box down and wiping his hand down his jeans as though to rid it of any bad juju. "While we're on the subject, no rocking chairs in our home either. *Ever.* Creepy as fuck."

"Duly noted," Rosie said, poking through the items.

Her hand got close to a small crystal ball on a wooden stand ornately carved with intertwined oak leaves and acorns. The ball itself looked like it was made from some kind of quartz, but the texture of the stone made it so that she couldn't see clear through to the other side. As her fingers reached out for it, a soft teal glow began to emanate from deep within the crystal.

"That one's reactin' to ya," said Captain Obvious.

Rosie very carefully lifted the small crystal sphere in one hand. It blazed into life, bright teal lighting up the area around them as she turned the wooden base over with the other. "Shit!" she hissed under her breath. "We might need to go and rob a bank first." She held the price tag out for Declan to read.

He whistled.

With a small sigh, Rosie went to put the crystal ball back on the table.

"What are you doing?" he asked her, reaching out gently to stop her hand. "That's the one—you saw it yourself."

"I don't have that kind of money," Rosie whispered, not wanting Francois or anyone else to overhear them. She carefully returned the crystal ball to its place on the table.

Declan's face was serious. He took both of Rosie's hands in hers, squeezing them gently. "We need this, for Maggie. Please let *me* buy it. We both want to do everything we can to keep our family safe. This is something I can do."

Rosie took a deep breath, considering Declan.

"Plus, it'll piss off my Da'," Declan added, dropping one of her hands to pull the price tag out again.

Done, thought Rosie.

Francois chose that moment to reappear, looking slightly panicked.

"Incoming," he said in a hushed tone with a glance over his shoulder at the woman who had just walked into the shop. "We don't want those mundanes knowing anything other than that this stuff looks cool."

"Sorry," Rosie apologized quickly, before blinking. "Mundanes?"

Francois nodded. "Non-magical people," he explained quietly.

Declan gingerly picked up the crystal ball—which didn't glow in his hand, oddly enough—and held it out to Francois.

"We're gonna take this one," he declared.

"Excellent choice, *monseiur*," Francois began to move, cradling the crystal ball to his side to protect it in transit. "Let's ring this up for you."

Francois turned his shoulder coolly on his cat—or familiar—as he bustled behind the counter. He quickly punched a figure into an old-style register, while Fabien jumped up beside him. "You know what you did," Rosie overheard Francois say beneath his breath. The cat meowed again, and Francois replied, "You were being a diva and you know it." Rosie glanced at Declan, who mouthed at her, '*Familiar!*'

"One crystal ball," Francois announced proudly. "Plus I'll throw in a woven carry bag, and a brochure about our upcoming drumming circle." He slipped a shiny brochure into a thick navy-blue bag with

Sanctuaire Sacré printed on one side, then handed it over the counter.

"Thanks so much," Rosie beamed as Declan dug his wallet out of his back pocket. She still didn't feel entirely okay about him paying for such an expensive item, but the thought of Cillian seeing it the next time he visited buoyed her determination.

"My pleasure. That'll be two." Francois's pleasant smile hovered beneath an expectant look in her direction.

"Two?" Rosie blinked. "Two… dollars?"

Francois allowed himself a small, genteel laugh. "Two *tokens*," he clarified.

Declan swore under his breath, clearly frustrated. Rosie looked at him enquiringly.

"Magical currency," he explained. He slipped his wallet back into his pocket, and Rosie glanced from it back to Francois.

"Can't we just pay with regular money?"

"*Absolument, oui*," Francois nodded, "if you just want the object on its own, like a regular mundane. If you want the magic *within* the object, then you'll need two tokens."

"Do you have any?" Rosie asked Declan quietly, even though she suspected she already knew the answer.

Pursing his lips, he shook his head. "Not here," he sighed. "They're all back home in Ireland." And then he looked like a lightbulb lit up in his brain. "But *you* have some back at the cottage, Rosie—remember? Those coins you found with Moira's diary?"

Hope swooped up inside of her like a rainbow. "Is that what they are?" she asked. "I didn't realize!"

"They're not that commonly used," he said with a shrug.

"Well, they are here," Francois sniffed. "We do things the *old-fashioned* way, I'm afraid." He glanced at Fabien as though it was a matter of some contention between them. The cat flicked its tail in annoyance.

"Well," Rosie sighed, her excitement at actually having tokens to her name vanishing as quickly as it had come in the first place, "They're no good to me in my dresser."

Fabien again had something to say about this and meowed loudly. He circled the arm Francois had leaning on the counter, his tail wrapping around his human's arm possessively.

"Are you sure, *mon amour*?" Francois asked him, leaning down slightly as though to 'hear' better. Another heartbeat, and then he smiled as though to say 'very well then'. "Fabien says that we can help you out," he told Rosie and Declan.

"Really?" Rosie said with relief.

Francois continued, "We'll exercise a transaction spell to deduct the right number of tokens from your collection."

Rosie was stunned. "You can do that?"

"*Fabien* can do that," Francois told her. "Though not

as far away as Ireland. And only for people he likes." Francois gave Declan a quick once-over as though to remind him he didn't.

"Thanks, Fabien," Rosie said to the cat, who simply looked at her with his big yellow eyes.

Francois pulled a small silver box out from under the counter. It was plain, and he opened the lid to show them that the faded dark blue velvet lining was completely empty before closing it. He then lifted a basket from beneath the counter onto the top of it and tipped it over so that Fabien could peer inside.

"*His* collection," he explained. They could now see inside the basket and all the little trinkets inside, including a jeweled ring, several plastic bottle caps, at least three candy wrappers, a few smooth rocks, and a torn cat toy. Fabien reached into the basket with one paw and gingerly batted out a tiny yellow rock and a candy wrapper from within. Francois dutifully placed them in the box and held it out to Rosie.

"Knock twice on the top," he said.

She obeyed, rapping twice with her knuckles on the old, polished surface. As soon as she was done, Fabien moved to tap the box twice with his soft paw. And then he let out a gentle meow.

Francois opened the box with a flourish, revealing two of the coins Rosie had found in the tin box that had once belonged to her ancestor, Moira Kelly.

"...*Wow*," she breathed. Even Declan looked impressed. "How much for the cat?" she joked.

Francois smiled, but shook his head. "Not in a million years." He reached to lay a hand on Fabien's soft fur.

"Thank you so much for your business," he continued in a brighter tone. He took the tokens from the box and slipped them into the pocket of his trousers. "Be sure and keep us in mind, if there's anything else we can do for you."

"Absolutely," Rosie promised. "Thank you, Francois." She added a look for the cat. "And thank you too, Fabien!"

As they made their way out of the shop, Rosie bumped into Declan's shoulder in her eagerness to whisper about the pair.

"Does he have a familiar just to run his shop?" she asked.

Declan shook his head. "The cat can't be his familiar," he said matter-of-factly. "He's not a witch." Rosie looked just as surprised, and Declan lowered his chin. "It was the cat that did the magic. And the secret room didn't light up until *you* stepped in. Francios is a mundane." He shrugged his massive shoulders. "Fabien must be bound to someone else, and by the looks of it, he didn't hold up his end of the bargain. Now he's stuck as a cat."

Rosie slowed her steps as realization sank in. "Oh," she said, glancing back at the shop. "How awful."

"It's more common than you think," Declan said. "The familiar thing, not the cat running a shop thing.

I've been in the magical community my entire life, and that's the first time I've ever been served by a cat."

Rosie's mind was still reeling when they got to the motel where she had rented them a small room for the night. As they went through the motions of checking, taking their overnight bags into the room, and settling in, she couldn't help but think about Francois and Fabien, and what big changes might be coming for *their* family if Maggie didn't pass her audit.

Declan, who had been busy in the bathroom for quite a while, finally emerged and came over to where she had flopped into a firm armchair by the window. She closed her eyes, letting the events of the day and the information she had learned at *Sanctuaire Sacré* wash over her. Her mind floated in a sea of questions—about magic shops, and cats-that-weren't-cats, and how exactly the crystal ball they had bought would even *help* them.

She sensed a stirring in the air only a second before Declan's warm hand reached out to take hers.

"Come on," he said softly.

Her eyes fluttered open, and she took in a small, soft gasp as he coaxed her to her feet.

It might as well have been another world in there. He had taken the small glass vase and the two drinking glasses provided by the motel and filled each of them with gently glowing magical lights not unlike the fireflies in their meadow back home. The bed had been turned down, and the pillows fluffed to perfection.

Rosie felt a little of her tension melt away. "Wow, Declan." She smiled wistfully, looking around at his handiwork. This must have been the most romantic that this cheap motel bathroom had ever looked. "This is an amazing gesture," she said, already feeling terrible, "but I really don't think I'm in the mood for it."

"Not in the mood to relax?" he asked, his arms circling her waist as he cuddled up behind her. He always smelled amazing and tonight was no exception, but her worries just weighed too heavily on her mind.

"It's a little hard to relax, given the circumstances."

"That's why it's all the more important t'try." He pressed a sweet kiss to her temple. "There's a lot goin' on, and there's gonna be even *more* of that once we get home. But ya can't pour from an empty cup—y'need to refill your own well, too."

"You're right," she sighed.

His voice was light as he murmured into her ear. "Can ya just wait a second while I grab my phone? I'd like to record you sayin' that for future reference."

She rolled her eyes, turning to face him. "Thank you for this. Seriously." She stood on tiptoes to kiss him.

He kissed her back, his hands slowly sliding up her back and over her shoulders until he cupped her face in his palms.

"You can thank me by enjoyin' a massage," he grinned, reaching to tug her t-shirt up over her head.

She gave in, allowing him to slowly undress her. His fingertips lightly brushed her skin, easing off her anxiety in preparation for the cozy bed and warm hands that waited to greet her.

"Mmm," she hummed with appreciation as she lay back, watching him work on taking his own clothes off, too.

He was utterly naked in a manner of moments, which wasn't a bad thing considering he looked like a cross between a rogue Irish highwayman and a Greek god. She allowed herself a split second to admire the view, before he joined her on the bed. The one that he would have struggled to fit into even without her already taking up prime real estate. He grunted a little and tried to Tetris himself into position.

"I *did* think about this before I made the booking," she promised, trying to hide her amusement as it became apparent that his feet would be hanging off the edge of the bed all night. "But this was the biggest bed they had."

Her amusement faded as he tried to make enough room for his large frame, invading her space in the process. Cuddles before sleep was romantic. Not having enough room to spread out afterwards was a travesty.

"Squish down a little, will ya?"

"There's nowhere to squish *to*," Rosie complained, trying to scramble away over.

He shifted with a grunt, making the bed wobble precariously as he reached for the change on the bedside table. Change was pushed into the coin slot of the vibration mechanism, and then it powered up with a slow build of reluctant electricity that sounded as ominous as a nuclear plant kicking into overdrive.

Rosie lifted her head. "I dunno if that's such a good —argh!"

The bed started to vibrate. Not in a gentle, relaxing way that would have further eased off her tension. Oh no. This was more like a '7.8 on the Richter scale' type shake. She clung to Declan, who glanced at the buttons on the vibration controller with wide eyes. He reached out again, his arm flung around by the motion of the bed. It took him several attempts to dial the vibrations down, and even after he had managed it Rosie wasn't entirely sure that she found the sensation *relaxing*.

She actually felt a little nauseous.

"You alright?" Declan asked, once the vibrations had dulled to a purr rather than a full-on roar.

"I'm all shook up," Rosie quipped, determined not to ruin his efforts.

"Sorry," he said sheepishly, throwing her a grin that was half apologetic. "Here—roll onto your belly."

Rosie complied, letting the warmth of his touch guide her as she wriggled into a comfortable position. She ignored the pillows by her head, opting instead to stretch out her neck and square off her shoulders as much as he could. So long as he was dishing out massages, she wanted to make the most of it.

He moved so that he was straddling her butt, which was pretty spectacular in and of itself. But when he began to knead the tight muscles of her lower back, Rosie felt like she might just start purring in tune with the bed. She let out a tense breath, drawing in a relaxing one as his hands worked up her back.

"That's amazing," she sighed.

He leaned down briefly to place a light kiss on her shoulder. "Good."

Silence reigned in the tiny room for a few moments. Declan's magical glowing lights maintained a level of intimacy within the room, shadows dancing on the walls with the flicker of conjured candles. He reached over to grab the small bottle of body lotion supplied by the motel, and cracked it open. Before Rosie realized what he was up to, he squeezed two large blobs of it right onto the middle of her back.

"Gah!" she exclaimed, jumping in reaction to the freezing cold liquid hitting her warm skin and then spreading as he rubbed it in. "What the fuck!"

His answering laugh was delightfully wicked as it filled the room, warm and comforting, and it tempted Rosie into laughing at herself too.

"Whatever," she said, trying for huffiness but sounding playful instead.

"Aww c'mon," Declan soothed, sounding like he was trying to cheer up a pouty kid. He took one of her feet in his hands, beginning to massage her tired toes. "How's that?"

"A little better," Rosie admitted, turning up the sass.

He pretended to sound hurt. "Only a little?"

"Well you only just started," she pointed out with grin he couldn't see. "Ask me in ten minutes."

"Ten minutes?!" he laughed, pinching her big toe playfully.

About ten minutes and two relaxed feet later, Rosie sighed. "We should probably get some sleep," she murmured reluctantly.

"Yeah," Declan agreed, holding his hand up to his face for inspection. "My fingers are all pruned up from that lotion."

"Let's hope it's just your fingers," Rosie shot back with a smirk, waiting for him to move so that she could roll out from underneath him.

But it seemed as though the bed wanted to up the ante. It began to shake violently again, even though any change Declan would have put into it would have long since run out on the timer. It shook so hard that the headboard began slamming into the wall with a rhythmic ferocity that made Rosie want to blush.

What on earth would their neighbors think?

Declan over-balanced, landing on top of Rosie with an "Oof!". Her breath was squashed out of her in an instant, and she tried to wriggle her torso out from underneath him so she could take a gulp of air.

By now the bed was going to town. The only time

Rosie could recall ever seeing that much action in a bed was during that famous scene in the Exorcist.

"Get—off!" she gasped, struggling to get her arms into a position where she could push Declan off her.

"I'm—*tryin'*," he grunted back, trying to steady himself on their bed which had suddenly become a wild bronco.

Rosie clamped onto the sides of the bed, holding on for dear life. Declan wobbled and then fell to the floor with a loud thump. He rolled to a crouch, lunching for the cable that plugged the bed into the electricity. He yanked it out of the wall...

But the bed continued its reign of tyranny.

"What the fuck?!" he asked, his handsome face flooded with confusion before he stood up and offered Rosie his hands.

"C'mon, love," he told her. "I've got ya."

Rosie tried to roll into a kneeling position, and while that might sound easy to the casual observer, she wondered if this was what it would feel like to try and stand on the roof of a moving train. She managed to get one leg underneath herself, and she used it to push upwards while she tried to get onto all fours.

A savage pain shot through her thigh and buttock, and she yelped and collapsed back onto the bed.

"Rosie!" Declan exclaimed, leaning over the rampaging bed to try and help steady her. "Are ya alright?"

She seized up, the pain settling in with a vengeance, pulsing angrily. "*Argh!*"

"What!?" Declan asked, trying to sit her up so that he could help her.

"No! Don't move me," she begged, in between gasps of pain and the loud knocking of the headboard of the bed against the wall. "I have—a—cramp!"

"A cramp?!" Declan looked perplexed. "We're not old enough to *have* cramps."

"Tell that to my ass," Rosie grunted, trying to massage her butt-cheek. She gave it a couple of seconds, and the pain seemed to ease off. Now it just came down to getting off the damn bed without setting the cramp off again.

"Okay hang on," Declan said, after assessing the situation. "I'm gonna lift ya off the bed. Ready? One, two, three!"

Whether she was ready or not, Declan slipped his arms around her and hoisted her through the air. In her eagerness to be on solid ground, she hit her ankle on the edge of the bedside table with a *crunch*.

"*Ow!*" She glared first at Declan, and then at the bed... which had suspiciously started to wind down again.

"I mean, obviously that was not part of my plan," he murmured. "Sorry, darlin'."

"I'm gonna get some ice for my ankle," she said, hobbling towards her overnight bag so that she could don her pajamas first. "Check that thing for batteries, will you? And put some kind of Do Not Disturb spell on it. The sooner we're up and out of here in the morning, the sooner we can start working out how the crystal ball is gonna help Maggie." She yanked on her pajamas, stood on her tiptoes to kiss him, and then slipped out of the room.

CHAPTER 8

T he trip back to Mosswood felt like half the time it had taken to get to Savannah in the first place. Rosie had settled into her space beside Declan in the truck, her side against his as she read stuff out to him from a magazine she'd found in the motel room the night before. She'd felt only the briefest pang of resurfacing memories as they'd bypassed Atlanta, and then before she knew it the highway had melted into fields which soon became dotted with errant pines that heralded their arrival in Mosswood.

Declan pulled his truck up to the curb outside Tammy's big, white colonial home. It was just one in a line of identical homes along Mosswood's most prestigious residential street—The Crescent. Before Rosie and Declan had even managed to get out of the truck the navy blue front door swung open and Maggie bounded down the path to greet them.

"Mom! Declan!" Hugs were distributed all around. "Aunt Tammy and I baked triple-chocolate-chip cookies, and had burgers for dinner, and watched a movie! And we did hair makeovers. See?" Maggie did a twirl to display the intricate braids woven down either side of her head. *Looks like Aunt Tammy had been on Pinterest again*, Rosie thought with a smile.

"Sounds like you both had a great time," she said, her arm around Maggie's shoulders as the three of them walked back up the path to greet Tammy, who had come out onto the porch.

"Yeah!" Maggie beamed, before catching Tammy's eye. "Show them your hair, Aunt Tammy!"

With an expression that was nine parts 'cool aunt' and one part 'dubious adult', Tammy mimicked Maggie's earlier twirl. Her thick hair had been scooped into dozens of tiny ponytails in a haphazard arrangement all over her head.

"Very avant-garde," Declan teased, with a sage nod.

"I don't really know how to braid yet," Maggie admitted, "but I think this look really works for her." Rosie lifted her eyebrows at the line that sounded like the two had watched *Project Runway* the night before.

"I love it," she grinned. "Why don't you go grab your stuff, Pumpkin? We need to get home."

"Okay!" Maggie dashed past Tammy, who smiled as she watched Maggie go. Rosie felt a sudden pang for her friend, who she knew had long wished for kids of her own.

"I'd invite you in, but I know you have fluffy friends waitin' for you at home. Y'all find what you were lookin' for?" Tammy asked, glancing between the pair.

"We found somethin'," Declan said with half a shrug. "Hopefully it gives us the edge we need."

"Well, good," Tammy said with a satisfied nod. "We had a blast," she smiled. "If you wanted to make monthly sleep-overs with Aunt Tammy a regular thing, I wouldn't be sorry about it."

"That's sweet of you," Rosie said, leaning in to hug her friend. "We'll talk."

"Yes ma'am, we will."

Maggie re-appeared with her school backpack and overnight bag. "All set," she declared.

"C'mon then, wee'an," Declan sighed melodramatically, "let's go sort these furry friends of yours."

"I was thinking," Maggie said as she half-skipped for Declan's truck. "Maybe we should keep one of them!"

"JUST GO ON AND PUT YOUR STUFF AWAY HON," ROSIE called to Maggie as she rounded the corner of the cottage. "I'ma check on the rabbits real quick and I'll be there in a sec."

She inhaled the sweet woodsy air that enveloped their little pocket of heaven. Mosswood didn't give out much in the way of carbon emissions, but up here on The Ridge overlooking town everything seemed fresher. The pines played their part, marching almost right up to the cottage in back with their fragrant needles blanketing the ground.

Rosie allowed herself a few moments of peace, letting her thoughts unravel so she could pick through them. She wanted to explore that crystal ball a little with Declan before they got Maggie involved with it. They needed to do regular homework, cook dinner, shower. It was a lot, and thrown in a handbasket with the worry of Maggie's upcoming audit with the COW, Rosie wished that she had either the power to slow or stop time, or clone herself in order to even stand a fighting chance of getting through it all in one piece.

The rabbits skittered to attention as she approached, noses twitching with the knowledge that it was almost time for fresh food and water. White fluffs followed her from a short distance as she walked to each of the water bowls. She hated to admit that they were cute, with their little twitching noses and silky ears. Letting her instinct get the better of her, she reached a finger out to stroke one on its head as it looked up at her and then boldly cleared its throat.

Rosie snatched back her hand as though it had suddenly transformed into a viper.

"Less time fraternizing with rabbits," it told her in a dry, obsequious tone that reminded Rosie instantly of the COW's High Inquisitor, Morgan. "And more time preparing Magnolia for her audit. You have a matter of days left, in case you had forgotten."

"I know exactly how much time we have left." Rosie didn't even try to keep the indignation from her tone.

She hadn't thought it possible for rabbits to ever be *smug*, but the look on this one's face proved her wrong in that moment. Its eyes narrowed at her, it's nose twitching to one side in an expression that rather closely resembled a smirk.

"Do you also know that at this very minute your child is breaching the Secrecy?"

Rosie's breath caught in her lungs, slowed to a heart-stopping trickle as a horrible feeling of disbelief mixed dangerously with horror overcame her. "What?" she breathed. The next second, her lungs kicked back in. She gulped a breath and took off.

"Strike two!" the rabbit called in a sing-song voice, as she bolted for house.

Just before she got to the porch, Rosie slowed herself down. If Maggie *was* in her room doing magic, then she wanted to catch her red handed. She stepped up onto the porch and slipped through the house, ignoring the echoing sound of Declan singing off-key in the shower. Maggie's bedroom door was closed, and an unnatural pink light glowed from beneath her door.

That. Little. *Brat.*

Rosie snuck up to Maggie's door, her ears pricked. Though the words themselves were quite muffled, she could hear that Maggie was speaking in this over-the-top upbeat voice. Rosie frowned. It sounded like she was doing a voiceover for some random infomercial. Slowly turning the doorknob, Rosie inched Maggie's door open so that she could gather more intel before springing into action.

The plan was good in theory, but a gasp escaped her as she saw Maggie standing in front of her desk, her arms both outstretched. Randy's old empty turtle shell levitated above Maggie, accompanied with the pink glow and golden sparkles that popped like fireworks on the fourth of July. The shell drifted around the room as though coordinated by invisible strings. Maggie had a huge grin on her face, playing to the camera on Rosie's cell phone which was propped up against the wall behind Maggie's desk.

"—and as the shell floats around in a mystifying spectacle of—" She caught the movement of Rosie opening the door wider and turned, a shocked expression wiping the grin right off of her face. "*Mom!*" she yelped, lunging for the phone and disconnecting the live video stream just as her magical concentration broke. The turtle shell crashed to the wooden floor with a heavy thud.

"Don't you know how to *knock?*" Maggie whirled to face her mother, but her bravado vanished as quickly as her smile had when she saw the expression on Rosie's face.

"What do you think you're *doing?*" Rosie stepped

forward, snatching her phone back. "The COW already warned us about you getting attention for your magic, and now you're YouTubing it? Are you for *real?!*"

"The COW don't even know about it," Maggie shot back, though her cheeks turned red. "You ruined my video for literally no reason!"

"Who do you think *told me* that you were in your room broadcasting your magic to the world?" Rosie threw her hands up helplessly. "They know *everything*, Magnolia. And it would be smart of you to start acting that way, instead of thinking that you know better than everyone else!"

Maggie's bravado faded. "They know?"

"*Yes!*" Rosie yelled, feeling the hot sting of frustrated tears pricking her eyes. "Why is this whole situation so hard for you to understand?"

"Why is this so hard for *you* to understand?" Maggie gestured at the phone in Rosie's hand. "I have actual *followers*. Do you even get how cool that is? No one would even *talk* to me at school before I started posting my videos, and now *everyone* does."

Rosie groaned, pinching the bridge of her nose. "You mean to tell me that all the kids at school have been watching videos of you using your magic?" The snowball that had started out with Rosie busting her kid doing unsupervised magic was quickly turning into a full-on avalanche.

"*Lots* of people, Mom! Not just school," Maggie

declared proudly, puffing her chest out as she totally missed her mother's point. "Worldwide! I have *fans*."

"What the bloody hell's goin' *on* out here?" Declan asked, appearing in the doorway behind Rosie with an old pink towel wrapped around his waist.

"That's my towel!" Maggie complained, dismayed.

"Miss Magnolia here," Rosie began, pointing an accusatory finger at her offspring, "has been *doing unsupervised magic* and then putting it all over the damn *internet*. And now the COW know about it, and have given her a second strike for jeopardizing The Secrecy."

"—they gave me *another* strike?!" Maggie asked incredulously.

"I have been trying to tell you how serious this is!" Rosie replied, her voice shrill and loud. She could feel her heart thudding in her jugular vein, her head starting to pound with the effort of trying to get Maggie to realize that this wasn't a game.

"Okay, okay," Declan said, gripping his towel and holding one hand up to try and infuse calmness into the situation. "Take a few deep breaths, love," he said to Rosie, sympathetically. "You're gettin' yourself all worked up. And you," he said, his voice carrying a note of harshness that he had never used with Maggie before. "You need to take a step back from the line of things that *you* want and think about your Mum. This isn't just about you, Maggie. Two strikes from the Council is a serious matter—ya mum's right about that.

You're skatin' on thin ice. We're both just tryin' to protect ya."

"No!" Maggie shouted. "You're both just babying me! It's not even like anyone realizes the magic in my videos is real!"

"That doesn't matter," Rosie tried to interject.

"Well, it should! If no one believes it's magic, why is it in endangering the Secrecy? They all just think it's special effects. You don't even *get* this stuff, so how do *you* know what I should and shouldn't do on the internet?"

"Maggie!" Rosie said warningly.

"Ugh!" Maggie crossed her arms in frustration. "I wish the COW would just take me away to boarding school already—at least then I'll be able to do magic without having you on my back about it all the time!"

"That's enough!" Rosie shouted back. Her heart felt like it had been filled with lead, as she levelled her gaze at her pink-cheeked daughter. "Magnolia, you're grounded. No electronics, no TV, no leaving without permission."

"What?!" Maggie looked as though she had been shocked beyond anything she had ever experienced. "That's so unfair! You've never grounded me before!"

"Well, you've never acted like this before," Rosie fired back, turning for the bedroom door. "Maybe this will shock some sense into you!"

"For how long?" Maggie demanded.

Rosie looked back over her shoulder. "Until I say

so," she declared, her final maternal mic-drop before she left the room.

"Fine! It's not like it's that different from how it normally is around here!" Maggie shouted after her, before slamming her door.

Rosie spun on her heel and scrunched her fingers in front of her as though grabbing thin air and then dropped them with an "Ugh!!"

GRILLED CHEESE SANDWICHES ON PAPER PLATES PRETTY much summed up Rosie's ability to parent by the time dinner rolled around. Maggie had been given hers to eat in her room, and Rosie sipped her wine quietly next to Declan at the table. Afterwards, the pair of them had retreated to the porch swing that had been moved onto the front lawn to make the most of the warmer nights, but even the gentle breeze didn't manage to work its usual magic on Rosie's nerves.

"I just don't know what to even do anymore!" she sighed, letting her head fall back against the cushion behind her. "Every way I turn there's something new to worry about and overcome. If it's not the COW, it's Maggie. If it's not Maggie, it's me and my magic." She closed her eyes. "Honestly? I feel like no matter what I do I'm bound to fail."

Declan let out a long breath beside her, as though trying to weigh the situation before chiming in.

He reached for her wine-free hand. "I know it's hard —especially when it feels like it's one step forward an' two steps back. But just think about how far you've come, since you closed the door of that cab back in Atlanta."

Rosie squeezed his hand lightly. "I know you're right," she admitted. "I just wish it wasn't so much of a damn struggle all the time, yanno?"

He nodded sympathetically, taking a swig of his beer.

"I want so much more for Maggie than I ever had," Rosie explained. Her heart ached after her fight with Maggie. They had never argued like that before, and it made her sad on so many different levels. It wasn't only the fact that Maggie wasn't listening to her or behaving the way Rosie thought she should. On top of all that was the clear warning bell that her little girl just *wasn't* a little girl anymore—she was becoming a young lady, whether Rosie was ready to accept it or not. Letting that thought percolate for a moment, Rosie heaved a sigh.

"I never want her to think that I didn't care enough about her to fight for her. I never want her to feel like she's only got herself to rely on. And I don't want her growing up in some institution."

"Those are all normal things for you to be worrin' about," Declan said, shuffling closer and resting his arm along the back of the swing behind Rosie, his fingers stroking her shoulder soothingly. "*Especially* growin' up in foster care. But I can only imagine that, as a parent, those fears'll *never* lessen. You'll always want more for Maggie than you got. You'll always want her to know how important she is to you, and how much you care about her. And while it's normal to feel that way, you also need to learn how to use those feelings to stay focused instead of lettin' them consume ya." He paused. "The other thing is that... well. Goin' to boardin' school isn't the same as being raised in an institution or foster care, love. I can tell ya from first-hand experience that my school years were an absolute blast—and it didn't make me love my parents any less for them sendin' me there."

The night intruded for a few moments. The sounds of early-bird crickets provided a base track for the hoot of an owl in the woods nearby.

"I hate it when you're right," Rosie admitted at last, leaning her head into Declan's shoulder. He smiled wryly, ducking down to kiss her forehead before he lifted his beer.

Rosie stared into the dark shadows of Needlepoint Woods. "If I don't focus on those fears, then I have to worry about an even bigger one," she added.

Declan pulled his head back so that he could look at her. "Which is?"

She pressed her lips into a thin line. "The fact that I don't know enough about *my* magic to be able to teach my kid about *hers*."

Realizing the depth of her self-doubt, Declan folded her into a one-armed hug. "You're the most powerful witch I ever met in my whole life," he told her. "I don't know that you need to worry about not knowin' enough magic. I think we just need to sit down—with Maggie," he added, "and work out how we're going to approach it. As much as I don't wanna rock the boat, I *do* think that she'd benefit from havin' a bit more independence. If we want her to think and act responsibly, we have to give her an environment when she can learn how to take responsibility for herself—and live with the consequences."

He was right again, of course. She didn't admit it this time, though, choosing instead to hold that card close to her chest. It wasn't that she didn't know she was an overprotective mother. That niggling thought ate away at her, too—usually in the seconds after she saw Maggie's face fall when another 'no' fell from her mother's lips. But even though she was secretly ashamed of trying to keep her daughter a little kid forever, she wasn't so embarrassed by it that she felt she could just give up the habit cold turkey.

"It's alright for you," she accused him, choosing not to focus on uncomfortable truths. "You grew up in the magical community, with all the advantages that provides. We had this dumped on us, and we've had to adjust."

"Don't make the mistake of thinkin' I had it made," Declan countered her. "I had pressures of a different kind. My grandfather and father have cared about nothing but fulfilling this prophecy for as long as I can remember. I went through my rebellious phases, too," he pointed out. Rosie thought about the whole Gemma situation, and the argument Declan had with his father in the back yard only days earlier.

Declan hesitated, as though trying to decide whether or not to say something. His conscience seemed to get the better of him. "Can I give you some advice, from someone who knows next to nothin' about parenting?"

"Please do," Rosie all but begged. "It's not exactly like my decade of experience is serving me very well these days."

"Whatever we do from here-on out, Maggie needs to be involved in it herself." He used his foot to gently push against the grass, swinging them gently. "This problem is partly of her making, and she needs to help us come up with the solution. But," he said, by way of a caveat. "*You* need to make peace in your heart with the fact that the solution might end up meaning that boarding school is the best option."

The very notion was enough to make her stubborn streak arch its back and hiss in defiance. Gritting her teeth, Rosie reckoned she wasn't quite ready to admit defeat just yet.

"I'll cross that bridge if I get to it," she said, looking up at the first quarter moon as she peeked down at them from behind a bank of wispy clouds.

CHAPTER 9

All night, Rosie dreamed about a crowd of strangers in black hooded cloaks trying to snatch Maggie out of her arms. No matter where they ran to or how well they hid themselves, shadowy hands still plucked at Maggie's clothes until it seemed as though they would finally win their bizarre game of tug-of-war.

She woke up feeling as though she would have been better off not going to sleep at all. Declan was already out of bed, and Rosie rolled reluctantly to her feet with her head shrouded in a fog of exhaustion. The scent of the coffee Declan was making in the kitchen did little to revive her as she headed for the closed door of Maggie's bedroom.

She knocked.

"Maggie? Time to get up." Rosie was already two

steps back down the hall when the muffled answer reached her.

"Five more minutes."

"No," she declared, the tone of a mother who was done negotiating hardening the edges of her response. "*Now*."

When she didn't receive verbal confirmation from her child, Rosie paused in the hall, her hands perching on her hips. "Magnolia!"

"*Okay*," Maggie grumbled from her bed.

The kitchen was her favorite place in the cottage after the master bedroom, but even its haphazard charm couldn't work its magic on her this morning. She stepped over to the toaster, fishing in the bottom of the bread packet.

"Here," Declan said, stepping up to take over. "Let me do that. You get ready."

"Thanks," Rosie said gratefully, going to grab her stuff for a lightning-strike shower. A few minutes later she was dried and dressed in her work uniform, one hand curled around a steaming cup of coffee and the other holding a piece of toast with peanut butter.

"Has Maggie had breakfast?" she asked Declan, taking another bite.

He pressed his lips together and gave a little shake of his head, as though not wanting to tattle but also not wanting to be on Rosie's bad side.

"Oh, for Pete's *sake*," Rosie sighed, abandoning toast and coffee before stalking off down the hall. She opened Maggie's door and stepped over to her daughter who was huddled under her covers. And then, in one fluid motion, Rosie yanked the blankets away and deposited them on the floor.

"Hey!" Maggie yelped, squinting at the sudden light.

"I asked you *twenty minutes ago* to get out of bed," Rosie hissed, "so unless you're trying to get grounded for the whole summer, I suggest you move your butt!"

Maggie glared, her hair a brunette fluff bomb. "Fine!"

Rosie wasn't about to be cowed by getting the evil eye from a ten-year-old. She held up her hand and began ticking off fingers. "Uniform. Shoes. Hair. Breakfast. Brush your teeth."

"Okay!" Maggie sighed in frustration, dragging herself up off her mattress.

Rosie strode back into her kitchen, took one bite of her now-cold toast, and abandoned it as a lost cause. She was in the process of main-lining her coffee when Maggie closed the bathroom door behind her.

Rosie hastily swallowed her mouthful. "Pack your bag, too," she called out, sounding more and more like a drill sergeant attempting to muster hungover troops. "Hurry up, or we'll be late!"

Declan had raised one of his eyebrows, and Rosie caught the tail-end of the expression as he turned to rinse his coffee cup in the sink.

"What?" she asked him defensively.

"Don't ya think you're bein' a touch too hard on 'er?"

Shots fired.

"She's complaining that I treat her like a baby," Rosie threw back. "You said she needs to be allowed to be more independent. Being grown means not having your Mom there to make sure you're doing what you're supposed to." She forced herself to calm down just a smidge. "She knows we have school and work this morning, and she chose to lay around in bed instead of giving herself enough time to get ready—and now she's made us late as a result. It's not okay!"

"You're absolutely right," Declan agreed, "but I think you'll catch more flies with honey, love."

Frustration bubbled inside of Rosie like a pot on the stove that was about to boil over. Everyone was full of advice about what she should do, but actually trying to save the day was becoming less and less of a possibility.

"Then next time I'll pour honey over her head to wake her up," she sassed, though admittedly it wasn't her best. Declan lifted a rust-colored eyebrow at her. "If she thinks anyone is going to be her living alarm clock and household maid in boarding school, then she'll have a rude awakening!"

Declan's brows were still raised, though this time it was for a different reason. He dropped the dish cloth he had just been using to dry his cup and held his hands up in surrender.

Maggie appeared in the entrance to the hallway,

ready for school. Her bright purple backpack was slung over one shoulder, and her face was caught in a sullen pout. "Can I at *least* have breakfast?" she asked, with attitude. *"Please?"*

Rosie left her coffee cup and plate on the counter. Maggie wasn't the only one who could act defiantly. "You can have some toast on the way to school," she snapped, going to put on her work shoes and collect up her purse.

DECLAN DROPPED MAGGIE OFF OUTSIDE OF THE SCHOOL, and then he and Rosie sat in silence until he let her out right outside the Go-Go Mart. Guilt was already settling in her stomach as they muttered good-byes to each other, but Rosie couldn't let go of the tension that had filled her up at breakfast. Blocking out the sound of his truck as he rumbled off on his delivery route, Rosie used her key and let herself in through the closed automatic doors.

The light in the office told her she wasn't the first to arrive, so she headed straight for the white counter to stow her bag.

"Hey Ben," she called. She grabbed her water bottle and made for the staff refrigerator in his office so that she could refill it. Ben was in his chair, as usual, and turned to glance at her when she stepped inside. Then he did a double-take.

"Damn, Rosie," he gave her a concerned one-over. "You okay? Looks like you had a rough night."

"Didn't sleep well," she admitted sheepishly. No woman liked to be told that they looked like Hell less than an hour after they'd dragged themselves out of bed. "But hey—thanks for noticing."

"Sorry," he said with a crooked smile. "If it's any consolation, I grabbed you a coffee from The Moon on my way in." He nodded at the extra take-out coffee cup sitting next to his keyboard. "Skinny vanilla latte, extra shot. Just the way you like it."

Her stubborn heart melted just a little. "Bless you, sweet child of light," she smiled. Declan had *tried* this morning, bless him, too. She just hadn't been in the mood for listening. She sighed mentally. "Let me just get my purse!"

Ben shook his head. "No, ma'am," he said, grabbing his cup. "My treat. Consider it a boost for dealin' with the guest congregation from LaFayette that are gonna be at the Church today."

"That's *today?*" Rosie groaned, pressing the back of her hand dramatically to her brow as she took a bolstering sip of coffee.

Ben pressed his lips together and nodded. "And we open in ten minutes."

"I'll go finish prep," she promised, turning to head back to the counter. "Thanks," she added over her shoulder, holding up the cup.

"Don't thank me until your shift is over," Ben joked.

His predictions were eerily accurate. Scores of out-of-towners in their best clothes poured through the doors of the Go-Go Mart, opting for the cheaper coffee vending machine and breakfast burritos on offer rather than a more expensive and time-consuming meal at one of the town's cafes. Rosie had to refill the beans and the water several times, while Ben hastily microwaved more grab-and-go food to put in the food warmers up front.

The early morning rush slowed down when the Church opened at 9, leaving Rosie time to put a new roll of receipt paper in the till and start stocking shelves. Maude had delivered fresh eggs from The Dames the day before, and the cartons were still sitting on a shelf just inside the loading dock. Rosie carefully stacked them on the trolley, wheeling them to the dairy case where they usually sat next to the butter, milk, cream, cheese and yogurt.

Her mind wandered to the growing problem with Maggie, turning it over and over as though maybe looking at it from a different angle would suddenly be the solution she was searching for. She grabbed cartons of eggs, stacking them neatly on top of each other. Until one carton clipped the bottom of another, and she fumbled. Panic flared in Rosie's mind. It was like what happened next played out in super slow-motion.

Rosie flexed her hand to try and simultaneously catch the half-open carton of eggs, and also stop any from spilling out—but her aim was off. She knocked it away instead and made another wild grab that sent the rest of the cartons on the trolley tumbling too. Before she knew it, a mess of broken eggs and gooey cartons covered the floor in front of the dairy case.

A snort of laughter made her look up, hands out to her sides and her shoes covered in egg goop.

"Clean up, aisle three. Looks like you have a real thing for getting *egged*," Matthew Bishop drawled from next to the small meat fridge. His blonde hair was scooped stylishly to one side, and his otherwise handsome teenage face was twisted in a sneer. "Guess some people just never *evolve*."

He was clutching a packet of steaks, a pair of sunglasses tucked pretentiously into the top button of his pale blue polo shirt.

"I've already had A Day," Rosie said wearily. "Why don't you put the steaks back and run along, or your dad'll be hearin' about how you took off school today. Okay?"

His smug expression, which was *so* like his mother's, vanished and was replaced with narrowed eyes and pinched lips... which was also like his mother. He shoved the steaks onto the shelf next to him, pushing it on top of stacked ramen noodle packets. He sniffed as he walked past Rosie, then left. Pressing her lips together to prevent a string of impressive curse words from flying out of it, Rosie gathered up what she could of the egg cartons, broken egg-shells, and raw egg. She grabbed the steaks, putting them back in the fridge before she went to get the mop and bucket.

After dealing with the egg disaster Rosie managed to finish stocking the shelves without incident, but Matthew Bishop's words echoed in her consciousness. What if some people *didn't* evolve—specifically, what if the reason she felt like she was struggling with teaching Maggie magic was because her *own* magic wasn't evolving? It was another worry to add to her already overflowing pile.

As she gathered up her things ready to finish work for the afternoon, Rosie checked her phone. When she saw she had a voicemail, she secretly hoped it was from Declan. She didn't like leaving things with him on a bad note, especially when he had only been trying to help her. But the recorded voice wasn't a sexy, thick Irish brogue. It was the same voice that she had heard from the enchanted rabbit.

"Tick tock, Your Majesty," it said dryly. "Better *hop* to it."

THE WALK HOME WITH MAGGIE REFLECTED THE DRIVE into town that morning. Maggie walked ahead, her bag on one shoulder and her head hanging low so that her hair covered most of her face. Rosie imagined that it was her daughter's way of trying to avoid conversation, and that was fine with her. She didn't really know what the hell to say anyway, and was happy to spend the walk listening to Mother Nature in case she had any tips, girl to girl, on how to deal with an unruly child.

On reaching Fox Cottage, Maggie put away her things and went straight out back to tend the rabbits. Rosie took the opportunity to try and relax in a hot shower, washing away the rest of the egg residue even if she couldn't rid herself of the icky feeling she had inside. Declan wouldn't be home for a few hours yet— he was rarely home for dinner on the days when he had to go to Huntsville and back—so it meant that there was an opportunity for some one-on-one time with Maggie.

But how would they breach this latest gap?

Maggie was already doing her homework at the kitchen counter when Rosie emerged from the bathroom.

"Need any help?" she asked lightly, aiming for the role of Supportive Mother.

"I think I've got it," Maggie replied, pencil scratching across the paper. "Thanks."

Rosie began to take ingredients out of the fridge, setting them beside a chunky wooden chopping board. Her trusty favorite kitchen knife would make short work of it all. She began to dice chicken, setting it aside in a bowl before rinsing the knife and chopping board, ready to prep the veg. She glanced at Maggie.

"You see to the rabbits?"

"Yes, ma'am," Maggie said, without looking up.

"I'm makin' chicken pot pie for dinner," Rosie added, cutting celery. "your favorite."

That finally earned her a glance and a smile. Rosie briefly thought about how much more like her Maggie looked with every day that passed. "Thanks, Mom."

"You're welcome, Pumpkin." Rosie allowed herself a small smile of triumph. She finished cutting up the veggies, turning them into the pot of chicken that was sizzling in olive oil and garlic on the stove.

Maggie's pencil hit the counter, and she sighed with relief. "Finished. *Finally.*"

"I have a surprise for you," Rosie said, glancing over.

"Really?" Maggie seemed to revive herself from the brink of Homework Burnout. "What is it?"

Rosie put down her spoon and wiped her hands on her apron as she retrieved the bag from *Sanctuaire Sacré*. She handed it wordlessly to Maggie, who set it down on the counter with a dull clunk before peering inside.

"A crystal ball?" she breathed excitedly, reaching in. As soon as her hand made contact with the crystal, the same teal glow lit up the inside of the bag and spilled out into the kitchen with a pleasant ambiance. "*Cool!*"

"It's not just any crystal ball," Rosie told her, helping her take out the stand and set the heavy sphere into place. "Declan and I went all the way to Savannah to get it just for you. Touch it."

"Wow." bending low so that she was eye to eye with

the quartz, Maggie gazed into the mystical depths of the glowing crystal. "What does it do?"

"It's gonna help us get a hold on your magic," Rosie told her, tacking on a hopeful "... I think."

Maggie looked up at her mom. "How?"

"Well, I don't exactly know," Rosie said with a half shrug. "It didn't exactly come with instructions. But how about you and I spend some time now figuring it out?"

Maggie's enthusiasm instantly waned. "I'm pretty tired, Mom," she complained. "We had this crazy hard pop quiz today for math, and I kinda want to go and chill out for a while."

"And that would be fine, if we had the time for you to chill out," Rosie explained testily. "I've been at work all day too, you know. It's not like I twiddle my thumbs until you get home."

"I never said you did," Maggie huffed.

"You don't have to *say* it," she said, striving to keep a handle on her temper. "You *act* like it. You're not the only one working hard on your magic, you know! I'm offering to teach you *while making dinner.*"

"Okay, fine," Maggie sighed, straightening on her stool.

Rosie resisted the rather strong urge to reach out and strangle her in frustration. Luckily for them both, Maggie decided to use that moment to plant her palms on either side of the ball. Sparks shot out from the center of the crystal, radiating outwards towards Maggie's touch like miniature lightning bolts.

"Whoa. That's... actually pretty cool," Maggie admitted reluctantly.

Rosie raised a brow, but thought the effort begged encouragement. "Let's see what happens when you slowly pour your magical energy into the crystal," she urged Maggie, leaning forward on the counter to watch. "It might need a little bit of you to kick in and start working."

Rosie felt the undeniable hum of magical energy beginning to build. Maggie's magic felt fresh and uncomplicated, sort of like a playful breeze on a clear spring day—carrying just the hint of freshly mown lawn. Rosie took a deep breath as Maggie gathered it in, holding it tightly the way she had been taught that day in the meadow. And then, all by herself, Maggie began to channel a small trickle of that arcane energy into the crystal ball.

The glow flared, like a flash suddenly went off inside the crystal. Rosie and Maggie both gasped, but then the glow settled down into a deep, pulsating light. With each slow pulse it changed color from teal, to a rich blue, to a royal purple, transitioning into a bright magenta...

"Wow," Maggie said, pressing her nose against the curve of the sphere as though she couldn't get her face close enough. "I think I actually can *see* something in there."

"Really?" Rosie leaned closer too, not sure whether she felt skeptical or relieved. "Slowly increase your magical flow—just like with the log. Niiiice and easy." She felt the flow quicken, and she braced herself. "That's it—a little more," she urged, "but just a smidge."

"I *know* Mom," Maggie grunted, trying to hold onto her concentration. As though proof that she was slipping a little, a 'blob' of magic spurted through the flow and made the crystal flare again. Tiny cracks were beginning to split and grow from the middle of the crystal outwards.

"Ease off a bit," Rosie told her, reaching to place her hand on Maggie's shoulder when Maggie ignored her. "Maggie, you need to back *off*—"

Maggie shrugged her off, roughly. "I *know*, Mom!"

"You *don't*!" Rosie insisted. "It's cracking! Here, just let me—" Rosie tried to reach around Maggie, intending to take Maggie's hands of the ball. But Maggie side-stepped her, taking the crystal with her. It slid across the surface of the counter, teetering dangerously before Maggie managed to settle it back onto its stand.

"—I can do it myself!" she yelped, glaring at Rosie over the top of the brightly flaring crystal. A loud *crack* popped from it, making them both jump.

"Maggie, just take off your hands!" Rosie reached out again, grabbing hold of Maggie's wrists. She wrenched them off of the sphere, but Maggie fought against her. Together, they knocked the ball clear off its stand. It rolled across the counter like a fancy bowling ball looking for a strike, and went right over the edge of the counter where it smashed on the tiled floor.

The supernatural glow left the kitchen, and the hum of magic in the air died instantly. Maggie's magic whooshed back into her, leaving her momentarily breathless.

"You broke it!" she yelled at Rosie, as soon as she could muster enough breath.

"Me?!" Rosie yelped. *"You're* the one who wouldn't listen when I was trying to tell you to ease up on the magic!"

"I was *doing* it!" Maggie protested. Her shoulders were slumped, and she had tears glistening in her eyes as she looked up at her mother. "I was doing magic on my own, and you had to butt in! You *always* have to butt in!"

"Because it was *cracking*, Maggie!" Rosie threw her hands up in the air, and then slammed one down on the counter for emphasis. The other pointed at the destroyed crystal ball. "That thing cost a *fortune*, and we drove twelve hours and spent the night in a motel just to go get it for you! When are you going to stop being such a selfish little cow and think about other people for a change?"

Rosie was *never* this harsh with Maggie, and the shock of it showed on her daughter's face. But only for a second. And then a stubbornness that was one-hundred-percent Rosie Bell slipped onto Maggie's face. She narrowed her eyes, and set her jaw.

"When are *you* gonna stop being so bossy and thinking you're always right?" she fired back, and it was Rosie's turn to be shocked. "You're not! You don't even know how to do magic properly yourself, and you think you know how to teach me? I'd rather learn magic from someone like *Gemma* than learn magic from you! At least she was powerful! All *you* do is fluff around growing plants and walkin' around at the full moon in your birthday suit!"

For a moment nobody said anything. Rosie felt like she had been slapped in the face, and being compared to crazy, evil Gemma was the last straw.

"Firstly," she said slowly, trying not to explode, "Gemma actually tried to *kill* you and I nearly lost my *life* trying to save you. And second," she spat, her anger finally getting the best of her. "You are *the* most ungrateful, rude, disrespectful child I've ever come across! Everything I do is for you—every damn little thing!" She punctuated the last four words by slapping her hand on the counter. "I go to work to provide *you* with a roof over *your* head, and food in *your* belly, and everything else besides! I worry myself sick over keeping *you* safe, and making sure *you're* happy, and trying to give *you* extra on top of all that! And it's never enough!"

Another silence gave the tables time to turn again.

"I hate you, and I hate your dumb rules about

everything!" Maggie shouted suddenly, her tears running down her face. "If you wanted to be a *real* witch then you wouldn't have to work! You could just magic up everything that we need! But I don't think you *are* a real witch—I think you're faking! I want to go away to school so that I can learn magic from someone who isn't just pretending to be one when she feels like it!"

"Go to your room this instant!" Rosie demanded. She could physically feel her blood rushing to her head, her cheeks bright red and her eyes brimming with tears that she refused to shed in front of her daughter.

"Gladly!" Maggie shouted back, "because it means that I don't have to waste any more time trying to learn magic from an *amateur!* There's only a few more days until my birthday, and then the COW will come and take me away for real school. And it will be the best birthday present ever!"

She stormed off for her room, the door slamming closed behind her so hard that it rattled the kitchen window.

As soon as she had the kitchen to herself, Rosie collected the dustpan and began sweeping up the shattered fragments of quartz from the kitchen floor. She hated that she had just said those things to Maggie, and her ears were still ringing from the things Maggie had said back to her. Was this the kind of mom she has become—yelling and screaming, and every conversation ending with a slammed door and bruised hearts?

She didn't want to believe that, but the evidence that had piled up over the past couple of weeks started to say otherwise.

CHAPTER 10

The light was beginning to fade out of the afternoon, leaving it more like a shell of the day it had been. Rosie sat on the small patch of lawn beneath the large oak tree in the front yard, her back against the tree trunk and her hand clutching a small piece of paper and Maggie's homework pencil that she'd left on the kitchen counter. When she'd been a kid, someone in one of her foster homes had taught her that writing all her feelings down onto a piece of paper and then burying it was a good way to move towards letting them go. She'd had every intention of doing just that, until she'd remembered that it wasn't just her feelings she needed to let go of.

Maggie was in her room, probably feeling pretty down, too. They had never yelled at each other like that, and the more Rosie thought about it the more she thought she needed to offer an olive branch—a real one

—instead of burying her feelings any longer. With her mind made up, she scribbled a small note onto the paper, folding it into a wonky paper plane. And then she blew on the plane, helping it fly into the air with a little bit of magic. It glided towards the back of the house, where Maggie's bedroom window was hopefully still open just enough to let it in.

It seemed like an eternity passed but Rosie just tilted her head back against the bark and closed her eyes, focusing on the sound of her own breathing. It mingled seamlessly with the crickets, and the sound of leaves swishing in the tree above her. After a little bit, the sound of footsteps approaching her over the lawn joined the chorus.

"You wanted to see me?"

Rosie opened her eyes and looked at her daughter. It was almost as though she was seeing her—*really* seeing her—for the first time in a long time. The rounded limbs that denote a child were gone, leaving gangly arms and legs in their wake. Her face had matured, too; it was more like Rosie's, with her cheekbones more evident and her hair scooped up into a ponytail that was like her mother's instead of hanging in girlish braids on either side of her head.

The person who stood before her was a young woman, now. Her baby had officially left the building. And in that single heart-stopping, life-changing moment, Rosie knew that she had to start treating her that way.

"Yes ma'am, I did," she said lightly, patting the grass beside her. "Why don't you pop a squat?"

Maggie got settled and Rosie took a deep breath as she tried to work out what it was that she wanted to say.

"You know," she began, "I've been thinking a lot lately. About us findin' out we're witches, and that we have this whole past that includes a crazy prophecy. We've been through a whole lot of change in less than a year, including everything with your Dad."

Maggie thought about it for a second. "Yeah," she eventually admitted. "It's a lot."

"It is a lot." Rosie agreed. "I know that it hasn't been easy to adjust, and I just want to tell you that I think you've done an amazing job at taking it all in your stride. Especially when you're also going through changes, too, and starting to become a young lady. I'm sorry that I didn't see that before now."

Rosie's words seemed to be magic of a different kind. Maggie shuffled closer to her, her smaller hand seeking and finding Rosie's. She held onto her kid, rejoicing in the connection. Everything was not okay, not even by a long shot. But this was the best start towards it getting there that Rosie could have hoped for.

"Thanks Mom," Maggie said gently. "I think you've done an amazing job too. I know you've been stressed out about how to pay all our bills, plus afford Christmas and everything." Her voice sounded wobbly, and she took a quick breath. "And now I've ruined everything."

"You haven't ruined anything." Rosie said,

genuinely surprised. Did she really think so? She pulled Maggie into more of a hug, nestling her cheek against Maggie's silky hair. "You can't ruin everything when you are my everything, sweet girl." Maggie lifted her arms to circle her mother's waist, and Rosie had to take a deep breath to stifle the happy tears that the action almost caused. She patted Maggie's far arm. "I'm just worried you don't *know* what you don't know about the world, Pumpkin. It's big, and it's full of people who won't look out for you because they're only lookin' out for themselves."

Maggie lifted a brow, and leaned back so that she could look up at her mom. "You mean like the COW?"

"Just people in general," Rosie shrugged, although the COW might have been at the top of her personal Shit List. "You know how I grew up in foster care?"

Maggie nodded.

"Well, the people who were my foster parents were supposed to be nice people—people who wanted to look after children who didn't have a home, and care for them because they didn't have parents who could care for them." She had never really spoken to Maggie in detail about her childhood. In a way, she had wanted to protect her daughter from knowing about the uglier side of life. But then, with a father like the one she'd been dealt, Rosie wondered how successful she'd really been on that score.

"There *were* a few like that," she continued, "but there were others, too. Some of them just wanted to *feel* like a good person, even if they weren't really. I didn't always have someone who had my back, no matter what. I didn't always have good opportunities, or ways to learn how to be better myself."

"You mean the way you do for me?" Maggie asked.

"Yes," Rosie said, grateful that Maggie was tuned in. "Exactly. Part of the reason I'm scared about the idea of you goin' away to some boarding school is because I worry it will mean you won't have that support when you need it."

Maggie thought about it for a second. "What's the other part of the reason?"

Rosie took a deep breath, and for a moment she thought about making something up. But then she met her daughter's gaze and told the truth.

"The other part is that because I'm scared I'll miss you too much," she admitted with a rueful smile and a quick blink to scare her tears away, "and I know that's selfish, but there it is! You're the light of my life, Magnolia Bell. Have been since the day you were born."

"If I *did* go away to school, you would still have Declan," Maggie reminded her, "and Aunt Tammy, and Myles, and Ben. And all the rabbits." She paused a heartbeat, and then grinned cheekily.

"The rabbits I could do without," Rosie laughed, "but I know you're right. It just wouldn't be the same, because no one can ever replace you."

Maggie peered at her mother knowingly, the kind of look that made Rosie wonder just how old her soul really was. "Me growing up doesn't have to mean that we won't be close. You'll always be my Mom. But I feel like I'm never allowed to do anything myself." She pressed her lips together, as though trying to decide whether to go ahead with her train of thought. "All the other kids are hanging out together, having fun, and making memories, but I don't get to do any of that stuff. And then I have all this homework from school, but by the time I finish doing it all I'm too tired to be able to concentrate on trying to learn magic, too."

Maggie picked at her jeans. "My videos were cool, because I could practice magic and it was still fun, instead of work."

Rosie suddenly wanted to scoop Maggie up and say how sorry she was, but then at the last minute she reminded herself that it would be something she would have done when Maggie was much younger.

"I can see how that would be pretty exhausting," she said instead, "and I do know how hard it would be to make friends when all the other kids have known each other their whole lives—but going away to school wouldn't help you fit in any better around town. If anything, it would make that side of things worse."

"But I would have my own friends at the other school," Maggie countered sensibly, "so it wouldn't matter as much. Friends who are magical, like me. People who would be able to help me catch up on how that whole world actually works, Mom."

Rosie nodded, and swallowed down the lump

growing in her throat. She met Maggie's gaze. "That's a good point. If you really think that going away to this boarding school will help you, then I'm willing to look into it with you."

Maggie sat up a little straighter, her eyes wide. "Really?"

Rosie couldn't help but smile at the sudden enthusiasm. "Really."

"I love you so much Mom," Maggie said, folding herself into the space under Rosie's arm. "That will never change, no matter what."

"I love *you* so much Magnolia," Rosie said right back, "and that will never change either."

There was a sudden sound of something scrabbling against the tree bark, followed by a light *clunk*.

Rosie pulled away from Maggie, looking around the tree roots that they were sitting by. "What was that?"

Maggie winced. "...I think it was my ring falling off," she said sheepishly.

"What ring?" Rosie asked, starting to brush her fingers over the grass.

"The key-ring that you gave me that belonged to Moira," Maggie said. She joined the search. "I like to wear it after school because it helps me feel more powerful."

"More powerful when conducting your unsupervised magic?" Rosie asked slyly, with a side-long glance at her daughter.

Maggie didn't pick up on her tone because she was

too busy looking for the ring. "Yeah," she said absently. "Can you see it?"

Rosie shook off her motherly consternation. "No. But it can't be far! It's not like its small."

After a couple of minutes of looking, Maggie let out a triumphant "Aha!" She dove for the glint of metal nearby, nestled in the fresh dirt that Rosie had been turning over the day the COW had first turned up. She held it up for Rosie to see, her brow creased with confusion.

"I don't get it," she said, holding the ring out. "This is definitely the same key-ring that I was just wearing."

Rosie looked at the item in Maggie's palm, which was definitely one-hundred percent a large skeleton key again, perfectly straight and slightly rusted. There was not a single dent in the metal to suggest that it had ever been bent into a ring at all. Maggie held it up and they both peered at it.

"Weird," Maggie breathed.

"No," Rosie told her. "*Magic*."

She turned to examine the bark of the tree, drawn by a pulse of magic just below its rough surface. Running her fingers over the texture, it wasn't long before she felt a familiar tingle in her fingertips. *Moira's magic*. With a deep breath, Rosie pushed her magic outwards to join with that of her ancestor. Before their very eyes, a bright golden glow enveloped the surface of the tree trunk, before it ran into the cracks of what appeared to be a door.

"How did you know that was there?" Maggie asked incredulously.

"I didn't," Rosie said, using her fingers to feel the edges of the door and then press in obvious places to see if she could find a secret door handle.

"Maybe we need to use this," Maggie said, brandishing her key. "Look for a keyhole!"

After a few seconds of close inspection, they found a long, thin hole in a knot of wood that looked just about big enough to fit Maggie's key inside.

"Here goes nothin'," she said, slipping the metal into place with an audible *click*.

The door shuddered slightly, as though the magic that made it possible was awakening from a long, deep slumber. And then it edged itself open enough for Maggie and Rosie to pull it the rest of the way open, revealing a dark, cavernous room beyond. It smelled like moth balls and cough syrup.

Rosie coughed, waving her hand in front of her face to fight off errant dust bunnies.

"Do you think there're spiders in there?" Maggie asked fearfully.

"Let's find out," Rosie said, nudging her daughter. "Why don't you use your magic to shine a light on the situation?"

Thrilled that her mom has asked her to take charge, Maggie did just that. One arm extended, she breathed her magic into the palm of her hand until there was a bright ball of white light nestled in her fingers. And then, with a cheeky grin, she threw it into the room like a live hand grenade. It exploded, showering the room inside the oak tree with light. After a couple of seconds, Rosie and Maggie both stepped inside.

It was surprisingly clean, for a place that obviously hadn't had a visitor in quite some time. A long shelf that could either be a bench seat or a low counter stretched around the whole perimeter, highlighting the fact that the room was round just like the outside of the tree trunk. A small school desk and a chair sat at attention in the middle of the room, facing a large blackboard that still had chalk in a bucket waiting patiently by its side. Behind the desk, built into the wall in such a way that it was the only thing that disrupted the shelf, was a large wooden door. It was painted a vibrant green, and had a huge brass knocker on the front in the shape of a Celtic knot.

Aside from the thick layer of dust on everything, it was remarkably well-kept.

The pair of them were speechless. They gaped at the set-up. Little round port-hole windows, which were identical to the one in Maggie's room, looked out onto the lawn but which were invisible to anyone not inside the tree classroom. There were a number of dusty items laid out on the shelf beneath the blackboard, and the pair of them started in that direction.

"Did you create this?"

Rosie whirled to see Declan in the doorway, hunched so that he could see into the room. It obviously hadn't been made with giant Irishmen in mind. He looked impressed, but tired from work. Rosie remembered that they hadn't exactly had a great morning.

"I wouldn't even know where to start with something like this," Rosie laughed, amused at his confidence in her abilities. "We found it—by accident. Maggie's key-ring unlocked the door."

"But you found the door!" Maggie chimed in, seemingly desperate that both her and her mother should have an equal share of the glory.

"Ahhh," Declan said, smiling and nodding. "It must have been Moira."

"I mean, she's the only witch we know of who lived here, so that would be my guess too—but why do you think that?"

"This is a fairy tree," he said, ducking his head so that he could join her and Maggie inside. "It's ancient Irish magic, supposedly given to us by the Fairy Queen when she lost a bet." He looked around, his green eyes twinkling with mischief as he took in the set-up. "Looks like good ol' Moira has come to our rescue once again," he mused.

Maggie's eyes lit up. "Yeah, Mom!" She skittered over to where the items were sitting on the shelf. "Look at this stuff—there's a witch's hat, and one of those old feather-pens with an actual ink pot!"

"It's called a quill, wee'an," Declan advised, joining her for the inspection.

"And there's this weird dial thing," she added, wrinkling her nose as she held up something that looked like an egg-timer crossed with an alarm clock.

Declan glanced at it and laughed. "Wow," he sighed, "My Da' used to have one of these that had been his when he was a kid. It's a magic-o-meter!"

"A what?" Rosie and Maggie asked together, dumbfounded.

"You slip it onto the handle of your wand," he said, grinning as he turned it over to show them the clamp on the back, "and it acts like a kind of filter for your magic. Makes it much harder for spells to go wrong, and much easier for the witch using it to control their flow."

"But we don't use wands," Maggie reminded him.

"Wands are more useful for beginner witches," he told her with a wink, "because they give you somewhere to focus your magic. Maybe we could find you one so you can use the magic-o-meter!" He handed it back to Maggie, who promptly flung it back on the shelf.

"I'm not using that thing *or* a wand. I'm not some kind of baby witch," she announced, raising her eyebrow before she glanced at Rosie.

"That's cool," Rosie announced, with a half-shrug. "I can use it then. What's the other stuff?"

Maggie picked up the stereotypical-looking witch's hat, turning it over so that she could peer inside of it. "It says Cognitive Conjuring Cap," she read dutifully. A tiny black spider chose that moment to scurry up out of the hat itself, over the ends of Maggie's fingers. She yelped and threw the hat away from herself, causing Rosie and Declan to jump back as well.

"Gross," she declared, brushing her spider-tainted hand down her jeans.

Declan looked at her. Rosie looked at Maggie. Maggie looked from her mom to Declan. "I'm not picking up that hat."

CHAPTER 11

There was just something about cleaning that Rosie found therapeutic. It wasn't that she enjoyed the act itself. Being up to her elbows in dust, dead flies, and cobwebs wasn't exactly her idea of a relaxing afternoon. Rather, it was the motion of her swipes with the broom to remove the cobwebs, the satisfaction of seeing the shelf in the oak-tree classroom dust-free, and the refreshing scent of fresh lemon that soothed her.

She worked methodically from one part of the room to the next, cleaning as she went. Maggie was sitting at the desk in the middle of the room, her ordinary homework spread out in front of her.

"This is going to take forever," she sighed, leaning back in the chair dramatically.

"I'm sorry you feel that way," Rosie said matter-of-factly. "Part of being responsible about your magic is knowing that you still have real-world stuff to keep up with, too."

"I know," Maggie said, straightening at the reminder that she wanted to be treated less like a baby. "I just wish it didn't have to take up so much time. Especially not when I could be using that time to learn magic before my Audit."

The kid had a point. And, moreover, if the Audit was a success and Maggie was going to be home-schooled for magic, they would need to find a way of coping with an ever-increasing workload as she edged closer and closer to high school. Damn.

"Tell you what," Rosie said, resting on her broom handle for a moment. "How about we make a deal? You can use your own magic to speed up doing your real-world homework, but only if you don't cheat on anything and you're still learning. Okay?"

Maggie grinned. "What's in it for you?"

"Attagirl," Rosie laughed. "The sooner you're done, the sooner you can help me finish cleaning and the sooner we can start your magical learning."

"Deal," Maggie said, knuckling down.

Rosie felt the telltale sensation of magic being gathered in from the atmosphere around them. Instead of watching with interest, she deliberately turned her back on Maggie and kept sweeping down the cobwebs from the ceiling. When she dared a quick glance in

Maggie's direction, she nearly burst out laughing. A steady flow of magic was being applied to Maggie's pencil, making it seem as though it was flying across the page at warp-speed. The rest of Maggie, however, remained exactly the same.

"No cheating," Rosie reminded her daughter with a faux stern look.

Maggie puffed out her chest proudly. "I'm not," she promised. "You can quiz me later!"

With a small smile, Rosie got back to her cleaning.

The next ten minutes breezed by. Maggie finished her homework and tidied it into a pile on the desk before she picked up a wet cloth and began wiping the windows clean. Eventually, the only thing left to clean was the grimy-looking floor. Rosie sighed, her shoulder beginning to ache from all the sweeping and wiping. She fixed her trusty broom in her sights. Collecting her own energy, Rosie flicked one hand at the door to open it and held the other out to her broom. It picked itself up from where it had been resting against the strange green door at the back of the room, and it began to sweep on its own.

Maggie and Rosie grinned at each other as the broom danced a waltz through the rest of the dust, not stopping until it had collected it all up in a huge pile by the door. And then, with a big power-sweep, it pushed it all right out the door and into the garden.

"Nice work, Mom," Maggie congratulated her.

"Thanks Mags," Rosie said, her hands finding her hips as a look of pure satisfaction settled onto her face. "I will *never* haul that clunky vacuum cleaner around the house ever again."

"A-men!" Maggie chimed, in a fair imitation of her Aunt Tammy, making them both laugh.

"Now for the fun stuff," Rosie said, wandering over to the blackboard. She picked up a small piece of chalk from the bucket next to it, and paused. Where did they even begin? Maggie was showing better control with her magic, and they really should start with simple things. She thought back to the first thing she had done on purpose with her magic. Looking back now, fixing a whole stained-glass window was probably more than she ought to have attempted. Suddenly, it was as though a lightbulb lit up over her head.

"Okay so we need to fix the crystal ball that Declan and I got you," Rosie said. She walked over to the box of broken quartz shards she had gathered and placed in a box under the shelf by the blackboard. "Or, more accurately, *you're* going to fix it."

"I dunno Mom," Maggie said, grimacing. "It shattered pretty good."

The box jingled with the unmistakable sound of broken pieces as Rosie carried it across the room and put it on the table. "It's not as hard as you think," she said confidently, before going back to the blackboard. With her chalk, she wrote a simple sentence. The sentence that had started it all for *her* really.

Fixing things is all about having a little love for them.

It was as true then as it was now. On first running to Mosswood, she had been wanting to fix her whole life and hadn't even known where to start. Declan might have thought he was teaching her how to fix a window, but what he had really taught her was that by having a little love for her own self, Rosie would be able to fix the direction her and Maggie had been heading. Now, as she smiled at her beautiful kid, she was glad to pass the lesson on much earlier in the hopes that it would set Maggie on an even better path.

But the blackboard, it seemed, had other ideas. The swirls of old-fashioned handwriting began to appear on its chalk-streaked surface, bleeding into focus as though the words had been written years ago and wiped off the board, until now.

If you had a little love for me, I wouldn't have been left here gathering cobwebs like a witch's britches.

Rosie blinked. "What the f—"

"Fudge," Maggie finished for her, gaping at the blackboard.

"I don't even know why I am surprised anymore," Rosie admitted, mostly to herself. "We're in a classroom designed for witches inside of a huge oak tree on my own front lawn, and a magically-shady blackboard is the thing that's gotta make me do a double-take?"

Maggie giggled. "Write something back!"

"Like what?"

"Here." Maggie jumped up from the desk, taking the chalk from her mother. She scribbled in her own child-like handwriting right beneath the original message.

But my mom doesn't wear witch's britches.

"*Magnolia!*" Rosie gasped, glaring at Maggie who was grinning from ear to ear.

The first words on the board started to vanish in the same way they had appeared, blurring out of focus and then disappearing altogether only to be replaced by new ones.

I know. I have seen many full moons in these woods, celestial and otherwise. But alas, fashion disasters are beyond my purview of expertise. If you intend to focus on more scholarly pursuits, however, I may be of some assistance.

The text disappeared and then reformed a moment later, this time with even more sass than before.

Certainly more assistance than some other objects.

"What does it mean?" Maggie asked. She inspected the chalk in her fingers and then flung it into its bucket as though she expected it to bite her finger any moment.

"It's just a spell," Rosie said with a laugh. She shook her head at the ingenuity of the magic, wondering how well it had worked to help keep whoever had been learning in this classroom engaged with their studies. "It's not wrong, though—we need to get a move on."

She walked over to the desk and took the pencil Maggie had been working with. Maggie watched intently as Rosie held the pencil in both hands and quite deliberately snapped it in half.

"Hey!" Maggie scowled. "That was my lucky pencil!"

"I know," Rosie said calmly. She put the broken halves back on the desk, walked over to an over-stuffed armchair that sat to one side of the blackboard, and sat back in it. She smiled at Maggie. "So, fix it."

Maggie stared at her mom incredulously. "But *you* broke it, not me!"

"But I don't care about that pencil," Rosie shrugged. "It's *your* lucky pencil. You care whether or not you can use it tomorrow, don't you?"

Maggie had crossed her arms over her chest because she knew her mother knew the answer. "Yes," she huffed.

Rosie watched her daughter, working hard to keep her face from showing her true intent. "Then fix it."

"*How?*"

Rosie tilted her head to one side, pointing at the words she had initially written on the blackboard next to her without taking her eyes from Maggie's.

Pressing her lips into a thin line, Maggie collected the broken pencil from the desk and held the two splintered ends together. She gathered her energy and then let it flow out of her, but the ends of the pencil simply repelled each other like the opposite poles of a magnet. Maggie looked up at Rosie, as though she thought Rosie had foiled her spell.

"You're too emotional," Rosie explained. "Clear your mind of all that. Put your love for your pencil into your magic," Rosie told her simply. "Try again."

Maggie looked taken aback by her mom's offhand tone, but she clenched her teeth and forced the ends of the pencil together again. This time when she focused her magic, Maggie's signature tenderness and girlish whimsy accompanied it. It flowed through her and into the pencil gently, knitting the wood and lead back together until Maggie held her lucky pencil—intact—in her hands.

"I did it!" she beamed.

"I knew you would," Rosie told her with a smile, before nodding at the box. "Now do it with the crystal ball."

Maggie put the pencil down on the table carefully, as though it might break again of its own accord. Then she cracked her knuckles and lifted the lid of the box. "This looks just like all our old Christmas decorations before you made them into the new star for our Christmas tree!" she exclaimed, glancing suspiciously at her mother.

168

"Really?" Rosie feigned surprise. "I hadn't noticed."

Maggie smiled and sat on the floor with the box in front of her. Rosie could almost see the cogs in her brain turning, as she tried to figure out how to have love for something that she hadn't been attached to when it broke. After a couple of minutes, Maggie held both of her hands over the box.

This time when she began to pull her magic in, Rosie could feel her determination. It made for a stronger, smoother force, and Rosie found her head bobbing slightly with satisfaction. But what blew her away was the way the Maggie channeled her magic back into the crystal.

Instead of it being the sweet, gentle magic that Rosie had come to associate with her daughter, there was more there this time. There was the enduring, steel-banded love of a daughter for her mother woven seamlessly into the spell. Rosie was suddenly overwhelmed by the sensation, tears springing immediately to her eyes the way they did when she was touched by a song that held too many memories. Her heart filled up with that expression of love, drinking it in.

Maggie wriggled her fingers as she worked, using them to direct pieces of broken crystal back to where they belonged. Before long a final 'click' signaled the last piece of the sphere being put back into place. But Maggie continued to pour her magic into the crystal ball, imbibing it with her own brand of magic and strengthening her connection to the magic that had been healed within the quartz.

When she eventually looked up at her mom, she was crying happy tears too.

"Awww hon," Rosie sighed. She went over to Maggie, who stood so that her mother could fold her into a tight hug.

"I love you," Rosie whispered against Maggie's soft, dark hair.

"I love you too, Mom," Maggie whispered back.

After a couple seconds, Rosie leaned back to look into Maggie's face. "Come on," she said, pulling them both out of the moment. "We need to work out what this crystal ball actually does!"

Maggie picked it up carefully, settling it into its stand on her desk. She took a deep breath and placed both hands on either side of the crystal.

Sudden, kitschy music began to play loudly inside the classroom, making both of them jump in surprise. The teal light from within the crystal got brighter and brighter, until it was almost blinding. Then with a sudden swoop, it narrowed into a magical projection of a plump woman dressed in a periwinkle blue suit. Her pale blonde hair was curled elaborately, Marilyn Monroe style, and she had a tiny little witch hat in periwinkle blue perched jauntily to one side of her head.

"Why, hello there Magnolia!" she said with a wide smile that was bracketed by her bright red lipstick. Maggie's name sounded like it had been dubbed into the projection. It was a much deeper voice than the one belonging to the witch, and her mouth just seemed to move without forming those letters correctly. "Welcome to Makin' Magic with Miss Maybelle! I'm your host, Miss Maybelle Montgomery!" The projection gave an exaggerated wink—which glitched slightly—before pointing at a sign that had just appeared in the air next to her with a *ding* sound. "Together, we're going to explore the wonderous beginnings of your very own magic. In today's introduction, I'll teach you about your F. A. C. E. That is, what magic *Feels* like, how to collect your *Arcane* source, the *Composure* required to—"

"This is *ancient*," Maggie complained to Rosie. "And I already know that stuff! Can't we skip it ahead to the good bits, Mom?"

"There's no need to be *rude*, Magnolia," Miss Maybelle said crisply, Maggie's name still in that strange, dubbed tone. "F. A. C. E. is fundamental to all aspects of magic, and it's important to learn. "

Maggie may have been turned off by the age of the video slash projection, but Rosie was riveted.

"The C in FACE," Miss Maybelle continued, unperturbed. "—is the *Composure* required to control your magic, and the ability to *Equalize* the flow of your magic."

It was at this moment that both Maggie and Rosie noticed the blackboard had words appearing upon it. Rather than repeating what Maybelle was saying, the blackboard had given alternative definitions for each of the letters, and E was still appearing in perfect cursive as they watched.

Farcical

Acronyms

Clowning as

Education

Miss Maybelle, noticing their distraction, turned to face the blackboard and settled her hands on her hips. With a click of her fingers, Maggie and Rosie gasped as the words disappeared from the blackboard. She turned back around and didn't notice the blackboard respond.

I can just put it back up here again, you ninny.

"The following exercises will help you to memorize these important fundamentals *and*—" Maybelle continued, ignoring the blackboard and raising her voice to prevent Maggie—who had just opened her mouth— from interrupting her, "—*improve* on any of these skills that you might already possess."

Rosie pursed her lips, and after a moment's thought she used her magic to drag the armchair across the floor so that it was next to Maggie's desk.

"What are you doing?" Maggie asked, looking from the chair to her mother.

"I could stand to learn this properly too," Rosie

shrugged, trying to seem nonchalant. "So, I'm gonna do the exercises with you. We're in this together, okay?"

Maggie grinned, nodded, and settled in behind her desk.

Miss Maybelle arched a manicured brow, waited for the pair of them to be ready, and then started the lesson.

CHAPTER 12

That evening Rosie stared off into the deepening twilight, cuddling one of the pillows from the porch swing. The screen door of the cottage opened and then closed, and Declan's boots sounded on the porch steps as he approached her.

"Here love," he said, handing her a glass of wine.

"My hero," Rosie smiled up at him, as he took a seat beside her with his beer. The swing moved gently under his weight as he settled, giving Rosie a moment to gather up her thoughts.

He pressed a kiss to the top of her head. "How did magic lessons go today?"

"Pretty good," she said, with a satisfied nod. "Miss Maybelle might even be able to teach me a thing or two."

"Whodathunkit?" he teased her, his signature crooked grin coming into play.

"Watch yourself," she sassed him back, sighing as she cuddled up to him. "I just worry that it's too little, too late."

His arm relaxed around her. "What do you mean?"

"We only have a couple days before Maggie's birthday," Rosie said. The productiveness of the afternoon wasn't to be written off completely, but the reality of their situation was setting in. "If we'd had Miss Maybelle and the oak tree classroom from the very beginning, we might have stood a chance. But now we're almost out of time. Maggie still has school, I still have work, and I'm still trying to get Nourish up and running with poor Tammy—who's already been more patient with me than I deserve."

Declan sipped his beer quietly, thinking. The night wasn't as cool as the previous ones had been, heralding a hint of summer on its way. Soon the lightning bugs would be buzzing across the lawn in the early evenings, and it made Rosie sad to think Maggie might not even be here to see them.

"Maggie could stand to miss a couple days of regular school," Declan mused. "Give 'er time to brush up on her magical studies."

"Maybe," Rosie agreed, feeling skeptical. "But I don't know that she would study as well without supervision. She's still just a kid."

"Well, you are only working mornings or

afternoons," he pointed out. "That means you have some time with her, though granted it's not as much as you'd like. But I could do some lessons with her, too, when I'm not working."

Rosie felt her heart squeeze, and she wriggled a little closer. "Thanks," she said, smiling sadly. "It's really sweet of you—but it still leaves gaps. No matter what, we can't share it all between us."

"What about Tammy?" Declan asked, an excited note in his voice. "She could help."

Rosie frowned in confusion. "But she's not a witch."

"It's not always about casting a spell you know. Like I've been trying to tell you, it's about finding love." He straightened a little. "You can teach her for the love of the things that you know—like nature, and moon magic. I can teach her about the love of the outdoors, and other things I'm passionate about. But we need more than just *us* on this path. That's why the Council want her at the school—because they have different teachers there for different lessons."

His eyes met Rosie's, and she could see a spark of wisdom there. "But we're *all* teachers in our own way," he finished.

His idea hit her like a bolt of lightning and Rosie straightened too, spilling a little of her wine on the grass.

"You're right!" she gasped, digging in her back pocket for her cell phone.

"I usually am," he grinned, leaning back with his beer and looking rather pleased with himself.

THE SMELL OF FRESH COFFEE FILLED THE OAK TREE classroom the next morning. Rosie carried in a plate of sandwiches just as Maggie had finished setting out coffee mugs on the shelf by the round windows. Declan had just finished adding the cream and sugar to the shelf, snagging a sandwich as Rosie passed him. The sound of tires on the gravel of the driveway made them all grin.

"They're here!" Maggie announced. If she'd been a puppy, she would have been wagging her tail ecstatically as she bounded out of the classroom and onto the lawn to greet her Aunt Tammy and Myles.

"Oh my goodness gracious," Myles said, his blue eyes wide as he ducked to enter the classroom. His jet-black hair was swept into his usual understated pompadour, and he wore a cardigan over a button-down shirt that would have made anyone else look like a grandpa but which highlighted his lean body quite well. Tammy was right behind him, a small straw purse hooked over one arm as she took off her sunglasses to get a better look at the place.

"Well butter my butt and call me a biscuit," she marveled, taking it all in before grinning at Rosie and Maggie. "How on earth did you—"

"Moira," Rosie said with a smile and a simple shrug that spoke volumes.

"Of course," Tammy nodded, smiling back. "Well. It's wonderful."

"Thanks, hon. Did you fill Myles in on everything?" Rosie looked from Tammy to Myles for confirmation.

"Yes, ma'am, she did," Myles said, looking as though it had been a lot for him to take in.

"Good," Rosie said. "Time's of the essence. We brought you here today to—"

"Sorry I'm late!" Ben bustled through the door, looking harried.

"But you're not late," Rosie told him. "We weren't even expecting you! I told you last night that I would fill you in when I got to the store for my shift."

"You guys are more important than the store," Ben declared, making Rosie wonder if she might pass out from shock. "I put a closed notice on the door and came right over," he finished.

"Who are you, and what have you done with Ben Major?" Rosie teased.

Ben smiled sheepishly.

"Right. We asked you all here because we need your help. You know the deal with the Council. Maggie's birthday is comin' up. I know it's a big ask, but do you think y'all could help us teach her magic in shifts?"

"See about that," Tammy said nervously. "You know I would do anything I could to help you out. But none of us are magical! How can we teach Maggie anything about magic when we don't know anythin' about it ourselves?"

"It's less about being magical and more about helping Maggie discover her passion for different areas of magic," Rosie explained. "And the rules around them," she added with a glance at Myles, and then finally she looked at Ben, "And how to keep her enthusiasm from running rampant with the ones she really likes."

If she'd been expecting some kind of collective 'aha!' moment where her friends suddenly knew the score, she would have been disappointed. Three blank faces stared back at her across the classroom, until Tammy broke rank to start making coffees.

"You don't have t'be magic yourselves if ya can teach Maggie about the things each of you love," Declan said, trying to break it down. "Myles—what do you love more than anything in the world?"

Myles suddenly looked as though that might be a trick question. His eyes flicked immediately to Tammy, before he caught himself and blinked. "That would have to be the Almighty," he replied.

"Exactly," Declan grinned. "And what does the Bible say about witches?"

"... That they're bad," he said awkwardly, toning it down for Maggie's sake.

"So," Declan looked a little awkward but gestured brightly anyway, "You could teach Maggie about the puritan ideals that led to the Salem witch trials, and a perspective on the history of witches."

"Which might help her understand why keeping things a secret is so important, and start her thinking about what her place within witch society might be one day," Rosie added with a nod.

"Y'all have your own society," Myles asked, sounding horrified.

Rosie glanced at Tammy. "Guess you didn't fill him in on everything, huh?"

Tammy shrugged helplessly. "Baby steps."

Rosie turned back to Myles. "We'll tell you all about the Council another time. Tammy—you could teach Maggie—"

"—all about my love for the kitchen, and home-making, and household economics," Tammy exclaimed, picking up the thread. "We could tie it to magical learning about potions, and the hearth magic you told me about!"

"Perfect!" Rosie beamed.

"And I could teach her about local history, maybe?" Ben asked. "I could give her more perspective on Moira, and the superstitions that abound in Mosswood and this part of Georgia in general?"

"Yeah, and you could tie it into maybe her starting to make a journal of her own magical learnings, similar to what Moira did?" Rosie added, making Ben nod enthusiastically.

"That's called a grimoire," Maggie said proudly. "I learned that from Miss Maybelle."

"Who now?" Tammy asked, glancing at Rosie.

"Well, doesn't this look... cozy," purred a voice from the outside door of the classroom. Morgan leaned against the open door frame, her black eyes gleaming unwholesomely. "Miss Maybelle?" she sneered, glancing in the direction of the crystal ball. "I didn't even know they still had them in circulation."

Rosie bit back a frustrated sigh. "Morgan," she said, wedging a tight smile onto her face instead. "How kind of you to drop in like this, all *unannounced*."

Morgan seemed to take that as an invitation. She swanned into the room, the bat-wing robes she was wearing flowing behind her like a cape as she looked around the gathering and then helped herself to some coffee.

"Forgive me Your Majesty, just stopping by for a little impromptu check-up," she peered at the residue on the blackboard. "Council standard practice—you understand." She paused a beat. "Working hard as ever to keep the Secrecy intact, I see. Who are all of your friends?"

"They're not my friends, they're our family," Rosie declared, her hands planting themselves on her hips. "And it's none of your business who they are."

"Mmhmm," Morgan hummed. She let her eyes linger a little too long on Tammy, who looked like she was clenching her teeth.

"Magnolia," she said then, as though just noticing Maggie was even part of the group. She leaned down with what Rosie supposed was meant to be encouragement, but which actually made her look like a predator. "How do your studies progress?"

"Better without interruptions," Maggie replied, deadpan, as she looked up at Morgan without blinking. Rosie wanted to cheer.

"Spirited child," Morgan remarked dryly, straightening up. She continued to wander about the room, looking at the other various items gathered there, her coffee cup held aloft. "I suspect she will do very well at Greybriar Academy."

"I have no doubt she would, if she were to attend," Rosie countered.

"We shall see." Morgan ran a gloved finger through imaginary dust on one of the round windows. "I must say that I'm reluctantly impressed with the use of a fairy tree to suit your magical education needs. However did you come up with the idea?"

"You might recall that my ancestors were Irish," Rosie reminded her, though she suspected that Morgan was already an expert in all things Rosie. "Their blood flows through my veins—and my daughter's."

"Of course." Morgan smiled knowingly. "We're well aware."

Rosie felt a chill envelope her. She could never really shake the thought that Morgan reminded her of a shark, and right now she felt like that shark was circling her daughter.

Morgan put down her barely-touched cup, glanced at Maggie, and then tucked her hands in her pockets.

"I will, of course, have to note the unsecured fairy tree and the mundanes breaching the Secrecy in my notes," she said.

"Unsecured?" Rosie snapped.

Morgan lifted her chin, moved over to the green door they had not yet investigated, and opened it. Beyond the door sat another house in another yard that Rosie didn't recognize, and her mouth fell open.

"Unsecured," Morgan repeated, the ghost of a smirk hovering on her lips to have caught Rosie out on fibbing about her strong ties to her Irish ancestors. "An acorn planted from this tree will create a gateway between the two. I suggest you see to it."

Her lips turned downward and she glanced out the doorway of the fairy tree, as though she had just smelled a fresh dog turd being laid. "Speaking of seeing to things," she added icily, "why are there still rabbits in your yard? There are only so many niggling little news stories that the Council's publicity has time for."

"Our magic hasn't worked on them," Rosie said, her defensiveness spiking.

"Your magic hasn't worked on them," Morgan repeated condescendingly, her eyebrows tilting the same way as her lips so that her face was a picture of unimpressed disappointment. "For Hecate's sake," she hissed, storming out of the tree classroom.

Everyone left behind her glanced at each other and then followed. Morgan steamrolled her way around the side of the house to the back yard, where the empty-seeming rabbit pen sat innocently in the middle of the small lawn. She held out a hand, gesturing to the pen with a flourish.

"I've been looking forward to seeing you in action, You Majesty," she said pointedly, a nasty little gleam in her black eyes.

Rosie resisted the urge to swallow her nerves. Nothing like being put on the spot.

She stepped up to the pen and planted her feet evenly apart, feeling the heat from the grass warming the bottoms of her jeans. With a deep breath Rosie closed her eyes and drew in as much energy as she could muster, taking it from the grass, the trees, the invisible rabbits themselves, and her own arcane aura. She held both hands out in front of her and released a powerful blast of magic that swept through the pen and rustled through the woods beyond the yard.

The amount of magic she had just used should have been enough to send an elephant into the cosmos, let alone a bunch of rascally rabbits. Feeling confident, Rosie placed both hands on the fence of the pen and leaned forward.

All of the rabbits were still present and accounted for. They were eating, cleaning themselves, hopping around... and Rosie was horrified to notice at least one pair doing what rabbits were known best for—and it wasn't delivering Easter eggs.

She leaned back, her shoulders slumping in defeat. As much as she didn't want to, Rosie met Morgan's gaze and forced a shrug that was more confident than she actually felt.

"See for yourself," she said to Morgan.

"I don't need to see them when I can still smell them," Morgan snapped. "Enough of this!" There was a sharp, sudden shift in the energy around the whole house. It would have been enough to make Rosie gasp for air, if it hadn't been lightning-fast. Morgan brought her hands together in two forceful claps that almost sounded like cracks of thunder, and then tilted her head at Rosie.

"For someone who is walking a precious line between being protected by the Council and being out on their own, you're certainly taking advantage of the benefits the Council has to offer, Your Majesty," she said. Her voice was soft, almost concerned. But there was venom seeping through her words.

She turned on her heel and swept out of the yard. Myles scurried after her, peering around the corner of the house, obviously watching Morgan go. A couple of seconds later, his face went pale.

"She just... vanished," he said, using his fingers to make a popping gesture. "Into thin air!"

Rosie leaned forward into the pen again. The rabbits had vanished, too.

"I think I hate that b—... witch," she muttered darkly. It was only then that she remembered the next problem on her ever-growing list. "Whose house even was that, through the green door?"

Ben and Myles shrugged their shoulders, but Tammy placed a hand on one hip. "Oh, that's Carol-Ann's. Haven't you ever been to hers for tea? Best sweet tea in the county."

"No," Rosie said thoughtfully, then glanced around the room. "But it looks like I'll be paying a visit."

MORGAN'S THREATS HUNG OVER FOX COTTAGE LONG after she had left. Rosie tried to brush it off in favor of magic lessons with Maggie. But when her daughter was getting ready for bed and the house was tidied up for the night, she couldn't help but circle back to the very real issues at hand.

Declan was already on the couch with a book. Rosie curled up next to him, tucking her legs up beneath herself. She peered at him thoughtfully. An idea had been forming in her mind throughout the day, and though she hadn't fully considered all of the particulars, she wanted to get Declan's opinion. It was just a case of how to raise the topic without upsetting him, or making him feel like she didn't care about his feelings.

"Can I help ya?" he asked with a smirk, his eyes still on his book.

Busted.

Rosie pressed her lips together, stalling for time as she tried to work out what she wanted to say and how she wanted to say it.

"I just feel like Morgan was so smug today," she said, worry coloring her tone, "that I don't know if the Council are going to pass Maggie out on her audit even if she *does* work hard enough to deserve it."

Declan nodded. Rosie pretended not to notice him dog-earing his page to hold his place before he laid his book aside.

"You're probably right," he admitted. "Morgan's got an axe to grind, it seems, and she's not the type to step back unless someone higher'n her calls her off." He fell silent. Rosie shuffled closer to him, laying her head on his shoulder as her mind searched for any viable option other than 'what will be will be'.

"We could try and butter up someone on the Council," Declan suggested, though his tone made it clear that by 'someone' he meant his father.

Her heart leapt, but a chain of doubt hammered resolutely into the ground kept it from soaring too high. "Ugh," she sighed. "We should do everything we *can* do, at this point. But are you sure that's something you want to try?" she asked gently. "I know how you feel about your father, and I hate the thought of having to suck up to him."

"I'm not thrilled about it," Declan admitted, leaning his cheek against the top of her head. He nestled against her silky dark hair. "But if it means the difference between Maggie passin' her audit and bein' taken away, then I think we should give it our best shot."

Rosie lifted her head and stretched to press a kiss to his lips before settling back against his beefy shoulder. "Yeah," she admitted with zero enthusiasm. "We should."

"I'll call him," Declan promised with a sigh.

CHAPTER 13

If everything else had given her pause for thought, Maggie's progress was the shining beacon in a dark room. Since being home 'sick' from regular school and being taught in shifts by her nearest and dearest, Maggie had blossomed with a speed and ease that made Rosie hope that they might just pull this off.

Declan's father had gruffly accepted their invitation to dinner. Rosie didn't know whether that was a good thing or a bad one, but for better or worse he was coming anyway. She wished she had a nicer home or better china to impress him with, and the emerald green cotton dress she had donned had definitely seen better days. But her hair looked pretty, and her makeup was on point, and that was as much armor as she could muster up under the circumstances.

"Mags, can you please set the table?" Rosie asked,

as her and Declan worked together in the kitchen to put the finishing touches on dinner.

"Yep," Maggie said. She collected four mis-matched plates and laid them out carefully, before returning to the kitchen to grab some cutlery.

"Thanks, Pumpkin," Rosie smiled tightly, looking up from the bread she was slicing as Declan as he waved a pan under her nose.

"Are these done?"

"Almost. Two more minutes," she told him.

He nodded and returned to the stove.

"Can we have soda with dinner?" Maggie asked hopefully, placing the salt and pepper in the middle of the table.

"No," Declan and Rosie said together.

A sudden knock on the door made them all look in that direction.

"That's him," Maggie announced nervously.

Rosie finished with the bread, but still clutched the knife anxiously. "Either that, or it's the Four Horsemen," she muttered under her breath, her stomach in knots.

"It's usually best if there are no sharp objects at any of my family dinners," Declan told her, deliberately loud enough for his father to hear, as he went to open the door.

"He's exaggeratin'," Cillian responded loudly in the hall, "always did have a quirky sense of humor, my boy."

"It's a miracle I ended up with a sense of humor at all," Declan muttered under his breath, as they came through into the kitchen.

"So glad you could make it," she lied to Cillian, hoping that she looked convincing. "Welcome."

"It's very kind of ya to have invited me," Cillian replied, holding out a bunch of flowers to Rosie. They were from the Go-Go Mart. Rosie tried not to react, but she was dying to know how Ben had handled *that* transaction.

"Thank you," Rosie said, flashing a soft smile that didn't reach anywhere near her eyes.

Rosie retrieved a bottle of Muscadine wine—Moira's recipe—and handed it to Cillian, with a corkscrew. "Would you mind opening and pouring this, while we get everything else ready?"

"I would be happy to," he said, getting to work.

Maggie was yet to speak, but her eyes hadn't left Cillian.

"So, what's new, Da'?" Declan asked a little too aggressively. The cork came out of the wine, and all Rosie could think was *thank goodness for that.*

"We need t'talk." Cillian looked first to Declan, then to Rosie. Finally, his gaze settled on Maggie. "All of us."

"About?" Rosie asked lightly, setting down the bowl of beans and carrots.

Cillian didn't skip a beat. "Greybriar Academy."

"Are you sure you're allowed to *have* a voice on the

Council?" Rosie went to fetch the mashed potatoes, while Declan wrangled the chicken pieces into a serving dish. "I'm not sure Morgan would like that very much."

"Ah," Cillian waved a hand dismissively. "Morgan's a bulldog."

"What?" Rosie sassed, raising a brow. "All bark and no bite?"

"Well-trained," Cillian said, his mouth hitching into a tight smile beneath his beard.

Rosie felt her spidey-sense tingling. "By you?"

Cillian began to pour the wine into the two glasses that had already been set on the counter. "The Council does what it needs to do t'make sure that their interests are looked after."

"I'll bet," Rosie said. She placed the mashed potatoes on the table and reached into one of the cupboards for an extra wine glass. She put it down on the counter in front of Cillian with a determined *clink*.

"Includin' breakin' up families," she added.

Declan had taken the chicken to the table.

Cillian sighed. He took two glasses of wine, holding out one to Declan and one to Rosie. "I didn't come here to fight with ya," he said. "I just came to give ya a different perspective, that's all."

Declan came to accept his glass, his eyes narrowed with suspicion. He didn't say anything, but a quick glance in Rosie's direction was enough to put her on her guard. She took her own glass and held out a hand to indicate they should sit for dinner.

"Even if I didn't know by legend that you and Magnolia had exceptional powers, I can feel it. I could feel it 'fore I even *got* to Mosswood with the Council. An' sittin' next to ya both is almost blindin'—aura-wise," he added with a rueful smile. Rosie looked from him to Declan, who gave a tiny, sheepish shrug as though to confirm his father's intel.

"Declan was always a rebellious boy, always pushin' to see how much he could get away with. Now that he's older, I can see that he wasn't deliberately tryin' to test me patience. It was how he learned about himself, and who he was destined to become."

Declan snorted. "Truth be told, I did do it quite often just to mess with ya," he admitted, making Maggie grin at him across the table.

"Magnolia has so much potential," Cillian continued, with a sidelong glance at his cheeky son, "not only in terms of power, but also in terms of what that power could do on a wider scale. Forgive me for sayin' so, but you'll never have the opportunities *she* could have simply because you weren't raised in the magical community. It doesn't make you any less of a witch," he added hastily, "on the contrary you have unique insights into a number of other things that give you your own kind of special strengths. But Magnolia would learn more than just life skills and spells at Greybriar."

The mentioning of the COW's magical school was enough to spark Maggie's interest. She smiled, presumably at the thought of going to a place that would nurture her magical ability. Cillian turned to her, playing to his audience.

"You'd learn about the history of our kind, the politics, the origins of our magic. You'd be taught how to apply yourself to all magical arts, and you'd develop ya skills in a cohort of other young witches who'll grow to become your network and connections." He smiled at her, his face taking on a kinder, softer expression that Rosie had seen his son adopt when interacting with Maggie. "One day, you could even rule over the Council itself."

Maggie's eyes widened, and she paused her mashed-potato-laden fork halfway to her mouth. "Over the *whole* Council?" she asked in awe. "Like Morgan?"

Cillian chuckled. It was the first time Rosie had heard him laugh, and it wasn't an unwholesome sound. Perhaps there was more to him than she had originally thought. "Morgan's just the High Inquisitor, but yes—I have no doubt in my mind that you could aspire to great heights."

He turned to Declan and Rosie. "You could both come home—to Ireland. You have responsibilities there to be taken care of," he said to Declan, before glancing back at Rosie, "and you could learn more about your royal line and what that will mean for both your future and your daughter's."

She couldn't help but feel as though Cillian had just spilled the tea. Was his real end-game to get Declan back to Ireland? Was he inviting her because he knew it was the only way to get his son home?

"Maggie and I will not be leaving Mosswood," Rosie declared. "Not for any reason. It's our home, and we've fought hard enough to keep it already." She glanced at Declan, and then back to his dad. "Declan can do as he chooses, but it's my hope that he would choose to stay with us."

"You don't have to hope for that, love," Declan told her, reaching for her hand on one side and Maggie's on the other. "It's a fact."

Cillian's face hardened, and Rosie realized that she'd been right. This wasn't just a 'I want what's best for you all' chat. There was an ulterior motive.

"Don't be so quick to—" Cillian began, stopping mid-sentence. His eyes pinned to the other side of the kitchen, and he slowly raised a hand to point. "What the hell is that?"

Everyone at the table swiveled to look at a lone white rabbit sitting before a fallen green bean. The green bean hung from its mouth, which moved ferociously, making the bean disappear more and more every moment.

"What's what?" Declan asked, glancing at Rosie in horror before continuing with his impromptu charade. "Must be a figment of your imagination, Da'."

"Very funny," Cillian said, throwing his napkin down onto the table. He pushed his chair out as though to stand up and handle the problem.

"I thought Morgan got rid of all the rabbits in the blink of an eye," Rosie said, not even bothering to hide the bitterness in her tone. "Where did this one even *come* from?"

There was a heartbeat of silence at the table before it dawned on her. Her eyes slipped sideways, narrowing as she looked at her child.

"Magnolia?"

Maggie shrunk slightly in her seat. "His name is Elsa," she blurted. "He's super friendly. I put grass in my old turtle tank for him, and he really likes it in there. He—"

Declan frowned. "But Elsa's a girl's name," he said, confused.

"Well he's too pretty to be Kristoff," Maggie explained.

Cillian banged a fist on the table. "*Enough!*"

Maggie blanched, and then leapt to her feet with a determined expression. "Don't worry, Grandpa Forrest," she said confidently. "I'll get him back in his tank right now!"

"What!?" Cillian gasped, though whether he was more offended by the rabbit, Maggie taking charge, or whether she had just called him 'Grandpa' was anyone's guess.

Rosie dropped her cutlery with a clatter. "Maggie—*No!*"

It was too late. In her eagerness to zap the rabbit out of the kitchen, Maggie had gathered and expelled a giant bolt of magical energy that sizzled towards the wide-eyed bunny. It surrounded it with bright pink light and golden sparkles, illuminating the whole room. And then, as quickly as it had flared, it faded. The rabbit was frozen in place with fear, staring at the humans as they stared back at it. After several moments, it seemed as though Maggie's magic had simple fizzled out.

"No harm, no foul," Declan said, clapping a hand on Maggie's shoulder while slipping her a look that said not to try any more magic for the evening.

But it seemed as though the damage had been done. With a squeak, the rabbit's ears grew to be ten times bigger than its head. Its tail followed; a giant fluffy puff on the end of its butt that was followed quickly by the rest of its body suddenly becoming enormous. Last, but not least, its head grew to size, leaving the whole creature looking somewhere between the size of a Great Dane and a Shetland pony.

"Holy shit!" Rosie exclaimed, gaping at it in horror.

"Nobody make any sudden movements," Declan warned in a low voice, as they all watched the rabbit looking at them in wide-eyed fear. And then some small, imperceptible change in the atmosphere flipped the creature's switch from 'bunny scared stiff' to 'rabbit-zilla goes ape shit'.

It launched itself into the air, knocking the light fixture right out of the ceiling so that it was hanging by a thread of wires, and landed right in the middle of the dinner table. Plates were knocked to the floor and smashed, food was trampled, and the bunny was soon covered in Rosie's signature buffalo sauce which Declan had smothered lovingly over the chicken. Feeling sticky, the rabbit shook itself like a dog and sent food flying all over the room—and the people in it.

Cillian raised his arm as though to thwart the creature's efforts, but Elsa seemed to be one step ahead. It leapt off the table right at Cillian, causing him to shout as it planted all four of its paws on his chest and then used him as a spring-board. Cillian grunted in pain as he was shoved to the ground, and the rabbit sailed back into the kitchen where it landed on the sink with a sickening *crack*. Water immediately burst up out of a broken pipe, spouting dangerously close to the wire of the light fixture.

"Get it!" Rosie shouted to anyone who would listen, picking her way out from behind the now-wonky kitchen table. "Maggie, you stay there," she added as an afterthought. She didn't want her kid getting hurt, and she didn't want her kid doing any more damage than she had already managed, either.

Declan dove, arms wide. He grabbed the now-soggy rabbit before it could jump off the sink, tackling it to the kitchen floor with a crash. In a flurry of buffalo-sauce-stained-fur and checked flannel, the pair of them wrestled for supremacy. The winner was declared when the rabbit managed to get one of its back legs free from Declan's grip, kicking him square in the face.

Declan immediately let go of the creature, pressing

his hands to his face. "Bloody hell!" he yelped, the sound muffled by his hands.

The rabbit was desperate by now. It streaked from the kitchen and into the living room, leaving long watery smears of sauce and mashed potato in its wake. Rosie dashed after it, her heart racing. She got into the living room just in time to see the rabbit using her couch as a trampoline, ripping the floral upholstery with each bounce as it frantically looked for escape, and found it in the form of her beautiful stained-glass window.

"Noooooo!" Rosie cried.

But it was all in vain. The rabbit smashed through the artisanal glass, landed on the porch with a thud, rolled, and then wheezed before it took off into the night.

Moments later, Declan came thundering past her, out of the door and after the rabbit. He was followed by his father, who walked calmly and then stopped in the entryway to look at the carnage in the living room.

"There's such a thing as tryin' too hard to do what obviously isn't best for one's family," he said simply, before he started to move towards the door.

Desperation spiked inside of Rosie, sharp and hot.

"I hope this won't affect your score on Maggie's audit," she said to his retreating back. "She's worked so hard for it, and she's really improved a lot since—"

He turned sharply, his eyes hard. "There won't be an audit," he growled. When he spoke again, his voice had a thunderous quality, and she could feel magic gathering around him. "This is strike three. Either Maggie goes to Greybriar, or you'll both be declared Lost by Banishment." Without so much as another word, Cillian let himself out.

Rosie took another look at the tragic state of her beautiful window, sighed, and turned to sit on the torn-up couch while she pulled herself together. But as soon as she put her weight down on it, it broke in two underneath her and she crashed to the floor, too.

"Fuck!"

CHAPTER 14

Declan returned from dealing with the rabbit looking the worse for wear. His hair had been even more disheveled than usual, his coat ripped in several places, and his face smudged with dirt. Everything indicated an epic battle, and Rosie could only assume that he'd been successful. He was in the shower when she stepped out into the darkness herself, her clothes left folded neatly on the bed as she made her monthly pilgrimage to speak with Mother Moon.

She felt an urgency to get to the clearing. It overcame her senses, pricking her skin from the inside out so that she didn't notice any of the usual natural wonders around her. She didn't hear the gentle cooing of the birds in their roosts, or the cricket song that usually accompanied her. She didn't take note of the softly crumbling soil beneath her feet, or the ghostly kisses of the Spanish moss as she wound her way through the trees.

Rosie was desperate to hurry along, but anything more than a fast walk was impossible without a bra. In a bid to quicken her steps, she crossed her arms over her chest and cupped a boob in each hand and upped the ante. The path she had worn through the undergrowth was faithful to her even if her senses were not. The clearing seemed murky when she entered it, like sea water that had been stirred up with too much sand. She tilted her head back to look up to the moon.

The sky was clear, with a smattering of stars sprinkled across its dark face like freckles. It would have been an exceptional night for moon magic, if it wasn't for the small, perfectly round cloud that covered the moon entirely.

Rosie stared for several moments, unsure if she was seeing what she *thought* she was seeing. Sure enough, the moon remained hooded from her view, the cloud dark enough that only peripheral light managed to escape around its edges. The result was the filtered light in the clearing, which left Rosie's spirits feeling foggier than when she had left the cottage.

How was she supposed to get the guidance she needed when even Mother Moon had forsaken her?

The long grass around her feet was still, and without even a breeze to comfort her, Rosie turned and made her way back through the woods. As she approached the cottage, she could see through the trees that the porch light was on. She'd deliberately left it off, so that it wouldn't disturb Declan when he went to bed. Her clothes were on the bed, too.

Damn it.

She seriously hoped that it wasn't Cillian waiting on the porch for her. Rosie hovered in the slightly thicker trees at the edge of the woods, reluctant to come out in her birthday suit. And then something caught her eye by the edge of her path. Something fluffy and lavender-colored. Her bathrobe was hooked onto a branch, and she smiled and sighed with relief simultaneously. Declan would have brought her clothes and come into the woods *for* her. Maggie was the only one who would have grabbed her robe out of the bathroom.

Rosie slipped on the terry-towel robe and wandered in the direction of the house. It was late, and Maggie had gone to bed hours ago. But sure enough, as she approached the cottage, Rosie could see Maggie sitting on the porch swing on the lawn hugging one of the cushions in a move that was startlingly reminiscent of the way she sat there herself.

"You oughta be in bed," Rosie commented, padding over the grass to sit gently beside her daughter. Maggie looked blank, as though she'd done so much thinking and feeling over the past few days that now she had nothing else left to give. Rosie knew that feeling. Raising a child was rewarding, but exhausting.

"I can't sleep," Maggie sighed, staring up at the

stars. "I can't stop thinking about how bad I messed up everything—*again*."

Wrapping her arm around Maggie's shoulders, Rosie lifted one foot up to rest on the seat and pushed with the other. They swayed gently, Rosie considering the weight of feeling behind what her daughter had said.

"You're just overconfident," she told Maggie, playing with the end of her daughter's long braid. "And impatient. That's all. Those are both things you can learn to control."

Maggie leaned, resting her head on her mom. "I guess."

"There were three other witches sitting at the dinner table tonight, all of which were better equipped to deal with a lone rabbit sitting on the counter," Rosie pointed out gently. "I'd like to see you learn to assess situations before you dive in head-first."

"I feel like I'm not going to learn that—and a lot of other stuff—until I have a chance to learn it firsthand," Maggie explained. "Maybe going away to school will give me the chance to be me."

But would it? Rosie's mind was fixed on the Cillian's ultimatum, and what that would mean for all of them. Was it really a matter of toeing the COW's line in the sand, or being wiped from their records? Rosie knew that Maggie didn't understand the weight of what she was asking for, but it was clear that her child was craving the sense of community that would be denied to them both if Maggie *didn't* go away to school.

Rosie took a deep breath and held it. When she let it go, she also let go of her control of the situation.

"I've been trying this whole time to do what's best for you and our family," she said quietly, "but I think that the harder I try, the more it feels like I'm going in the opposite direction to where we wanna be." She squeezed Maggie and hugged her close.

"So, can I go to Greybriar?" Maggie asked hopefully. "Please, Mom? Can we at least *try* it?"

Rosie looked over at her daughter and nodded slowly. "Okay." She pressed a kiss to the top of her daughter's head, determined to sit with her and enjoy her closeness a little longer.

THE NEXT MORNING, MAGGIE CAMPED HERSELF OUT ON the porch with a small bag bearing her most important possessions: several stones she had collected from the woods, her two favorite books, and her best clothes. Her regular everyday items were in it as well, but the Council had been very specific about what she would and would not need to bring with her to school. Declan had contacted his father the night before, who had made all the necessary arrangements.

"I can't believe they're coming to collect her today," Rosie lamented, watching Maggie pacing on the porch through the repaired living room window.

"They're scared you're going to change your mind,"

Declan half-laughed. He came to stand behind Rosie, sliding his strong arms around her waist like the best kind of security blanket. He smelled like fresh forest air and woodsmoke, and Rosie breathed him in deeply before sighing.

"They oughta be," she admitted softly. "I'm half tempted to lock her in the garden shed and not let her out until she's eighteen."

"I bet she'd be *really* well-adjusted," he teased, resting his chin on her shoulder as they watched Maggie.

Rosie didn't know whether to be happy for her daughter, or heartbroken for herself. "She's so excited."

"It's an adventure," Declan agreed, a wistful smile in his tone.

"It didn't feel that way for me when I was her age," Rosie reminisced. "Any time I had to pack my suitcase and wait for a cab, I knew it meant a new family to meet and a new set of rules to live by."

Declan took a minute to appreciate her perspective before he leaned in and kissed her cheek. "She'll be fine," he promised. "Trust me, she's going to love it."

Rosie pressed her lips together in a strained smile. "I hope so. Especially after what it's costing your father. I promise I'll pay back every penny."

"Hey, he wanted Maggie to get a good education, and he was happy to pay for it."

Rosie turned her head to kiss *his* cheek. "Thank you," she murmured, then shook her head slightly as though to wake herself up from a particularly vivid dream. "I still can't believe my baby's going away to school."

"C'mon," Declan said, unwinding himself from the cuddle and taking Rosie's hand instead. "Let's go wait with her, eh?"

They stepped out onto the porch, and Rosie had a sudden flash of inspiration. "I'll catch up," she promised. As Declan took Maggie to look for butterflies to distract her from waiting, Rosie slipped around the house and into the greenhouse.

She grabbed an old tin can she'd saved, hastily filled it with soil and added her home-made compost. Then she plucked an acorn from a small basket on her potting bench, pressing it into the soil mix. Her arcane energy was easily summoned. She channeled it down and through her fingertips as she kept them just lightly touching the top of the soil. A thin green curl burst up through the dark soil. It was soon joined by a tiny leaf that grew, and then another. In a matter of moments, Rosie had herself a fairy tree sapling.

Who knew that Morgan could be so inadvertently *helpful?*

She cradled the sapling in her hands as she rejoined Declan and Maggie, presenting the tin to her daughter.

"Is that—?" Maggie asked, wide-eyed.

"Yep," Rosie told her, pulling her in for a hug. "Keep it safe and take care of it. It will be a while before it can be a portal, I'm guessing, but it's something to remind you of home until then."

"Thanks, Mom," Maggie beamed.

As if on cue a strong breeze flew up over the lawn towards the cottage, heralding the arrival of the Council. Rosie and Declan watched Morgan, Hella, and Cillian step out from around the back of the original fairy tree, Morgan giving it a sidelong glance as though wondering whether Rosie had sealed off its portal yet. When she noticed the sapling that Maggie was holding, she scowled as though displeased but she held her tongue in an unspoken truce with Rosie, who was bending to Council wishes.

"Your Majesties," she called as she approached. Her flat, black eyes coasted to take in Maggie as she came down the porch steps, her bag over her shoulder. "Good morning Magnolia."

"Good morning," Maggie replied with wary politeness.

Hella smiled, her white teeth all the whiter thanks to the dark plum lipstick she was wearing. "Ready to go, baby-girl?"

"Almost." Maggie turned and walked quickly over to Rosie. They hugged tightly, rocking slightly from side to side. "I love you so much, and I promise to call. Not every day, maybe—but at least once a week!"

Rosie allowed herself a small chuckle as she desperately fought back the tears that threatened to fall. "You be on your best behavior," she told Maggie. "And if you have any problems, you call me, okay? Anytime, day or night."

"Okay," Maggie promised. She reached up to kiss Rosie. "Bye, Mom."

"Bye, Pumpkin," Rosie replied, kissing Maggie back. And then, just like that, Maggie was no longer a little girl in her arms anymore.

"Bye Declan!" she said, giving him a brief hug too.

"See ya, wee'an," he grinned down at her. "Have fun!"

Maggie beamed. "I will!"

Maggie wandered over to where the Council were waiting. Cillian nodded, just one, in Rosie's direction. She inclined her chin but didn't say anything.

"We will be in regular contact with you regarding her progress," Morgan informed her, "and anything else you need to be aware of."

"Bye!" Rosie said one more time, as the small group started to walk away.

"Bye!" Maggie called back, before she started to talk excitedly to Hella about something. The group disappeared back behind the tree, and the reversal of the breeze that had arrived with them told Rosie and Declan that they were gone.

Rosie sighed. "Welp," she said, putting her hands on her hips and throwing Declan a hopeless look. "*Now* what?"

CHAPTER 15

Declan had taken off for work not long after Maggie had left for Greybriar, which left Rosie at a loss. Normally she would have relished having the morning to herself, but those had been the days where Maggie was just down the road at Mosswood Elementary and not in a magical academy miles away from her. She chose to focus on what she *could*—cleaning.

By the time she had cleaned Maggie's room, tidied the kitchen, done the laundry and hung it out to dry *and* magically set the broom to sweeping all the floors, Rosie was glad that she was almost due for her shift at the Go-Go. She got dressed and walked into town early, hoping to enjoy a bit of fresh air. But even that seemed lackluster, because she usually took those walks with Maggie.

She made her way past the old Hayes Sugar and

Syrup building, past the Beep'n Sleep, and past Granny's Diner with its huge sign out front. It would have been a blessing if her mind had been full of thoughts for a change; on this occasion, Rosie felt oddly blank. Ben was behind the counter when she got to the Go-Go, scrolling through his phone with a bored expression. He looked up and smiled with relief when he saw it was her.

"Oh, thank God you're early," he told her, perking up visibly. "It's been slower than a wet week in here today!"

Rosie groaned. "I was hoping that this would be a distraction, not a drag," she replied, stowing her purse under the counter.

"What're you needin' a distraction from?" Ben asked, slipping his phone into the back pocket of his jeans and leaning forward on the counter with interest.

"Maggie's gone away to that school," she said quietly, unsure if there were any customers in the store. "She left this morning. It was the best thing for her."

Rosie didn't know whether she was trying to convince Ben, or herself.

Ben blinked. "Are you okay?"

Rosie nodded hastily, turning her head away so that she could stifle the tears that sprang into her eyes at his question before he could see them. She turned back to him, her face schooled into a more accepting expression.

"It's fine," she lied. "I'm just at odds without her, is

all. Even though she would have been at school today anyway, it's tough to know that she won't be there for dinner tonight."

"I'm always available for home-cooked meals," Ben teased.

Rosie laughed. "Bet you are."

Having her chosen family in Mosswood was one of the things that made her life there so good. She'd never felt like she belonged in a place more, and it was all down to the amazing people she was surrounded by.

"Just puttin' it out there." He shrugged, trying to keep the mood light. "Have you thought about talkin' to someone about it all?"

She almost laughed out loud at the suggestion. All she had done for the past week and a half was talk, think, and feel the whole situation.

"Declan and I have spoken about it," she said, "and I've talked to Tammy. And now you." Rosie forced a smile onto her face, coaxing back that feeling of gratitude for her loved ones. "I'm lucky to have the best friends in the world."

"You are," Ben smiled back, not even attempting modesty. "But I mean have you spoken to someone... impartial."

The question made Rosie stop and think. "Like a counsellor?" she asked.

"It couldn't hurt," Ben said. He began to restock the chewing gum stand on top of the counter. Rosie could tell it was more so his hands were busy, rather than him not taking the conversation seriously. "Even if it's just to get stuff off your chest. There's a counselling service available through the Church. Non-denominational," he added.

Rosie blinked at him. "I..." she began, trying to find the words. "I don't think that would be a great idea at the moment, but maybe another time," she told him.

"I'm sure it feels that way," Ben said gently, "but you really seem like it might be something that could help you make sense of everything."

"How?" Rosie asked, perhaps a little more harshly than she'd intended. "It's not like I can talk about magical stuff to a counsellor. And I'm sick of tip-toeing around the whos, whats, whens, wheres and whys with everybody!"

Ben leaned back a little. His eyes felt more piercing than they usually were, somehow, and he lifted both eyebrows and huffed like he was surprised at her.

"Okay, out."

Rosie felt the color drain from her face. "Pardon me?"

"You heard me," Ben reiterated, flapping a hand her way. "Out! You need to go and think things over, and you're not going to be able to think about anything as long as you're here working."

"You can't just kick me out during my shift," Rosie complained, standing her ground now that she knew she wasn't being fired. "I need the money!"

"I'll pay you to go take a walk," he countered,

sounding every bit like an older brother who knew better.

Not wanting to be alone had been why Rosie had looked forward to work so much that day in the first place. Being forced to go for a walk by herself would be decimating that plan of attack.

"You can't just pay me for walking around town," she argued, one hand on her hip. "That's not fair to you."

"Well, I'm not paying you anything unless you *do* go for a walk," he shot back, "so you better get to steppin'."

Rosie glared at him, but he refused to budge and stared right back. With a huff of her own she bent to collect the bag she had recently stowed.

"Don't forget your latte," Ben told her pleasantly.

BEING TURNED LOOSE ON THE STREETS OF MOSSWOOD with nothing but her thoughts for company was about as wonderful as finding a palmetto bug in her pillowcase. Both left her feeling completely grossed out, even if it was in totally different ways. The sneakers she wore to work for their comfort and light weight felt like they were made of construction-grade concrete as she plodded down Main Street, keeping an eye out for any kind of distraction that she could manage.

She made it as far as Lee Street without seeing

anyone she knew and Carol-Ann's realty office was closed up, indicating that the hawk-faced woman was either showing a property or out at one of her other businesses checking up on things. Rosie crossed the street and wandered into the park instead.

It was a beautiful spring day, all crisp white clouds and bright green grass. She walked the length of the path that led from one end of the park to the other, ending up at the fountain and statue that was an ode to the town's founder—General Beaufort Moss. He looked down at her with a sour expression captured forever in some kind of fake bronze, looking far too above himself for a man whose town could even spring for a real bronze casting of him.

Rosie deposited her empty coffee cup in a bin and carried on across another street, wandering in the direction of the riverfront. She passed by the playground where she had spent countless hours with Maggie since their arrival in Mosswood. She slowed her pace, thinking of racing Maggie to the top of the climbing frame. Would Maggie even want to play on the playground equipment when she came back from boarding school in the summer?

She moved over to sit on the swing she usually occupied whenever they paid the playground a visit. Swinging gently, her mind inevitably went to all the other things Maggie might not want to do when she got back. Right now she was still small enough that she didn't mind holding Rosie's hand when they were walking. Were those days behind them, too? She didn't know how she was supposed to just accept that she would miss major parts of her daughter growing into a young woman, without the comfort blanket of being able to hold on to the last memories of those precious childhood years.

She wouldn't want to feed the ducks in the summer. She wouldn't want to read a book at bedtime with her Mom. She wouldn't want to build pillow forts anymore. And while Rosie knew deep down in her heart that those things would be replaced with *other* things—like talking about boys, and doing each other's nails or hair—the baby things were precious. Losing them meant she was losing part of herself as a mother; the part where her child actually *relied* on her.

Tears streaked down her cheeks, and she sniffled and swiped them away before taking a deep breath. She stood up, leaving the swing still moving slightly behind her as though the ghosts of her past weren't ready to let her go just yet.

She wandered back through the park towards the Go-Go Mart, but as she crested the final hill up towards Lee Street she noticed the steeple of the Church standing tall against the bright spring sky. She wasn't sure she'd been gone long enough for Ben to seriously contemplate letting her back into work, and if nothing else praying would certainly be a distraction.

Couldn't hurt.

Her feet did the rest of the hard work. Before she

knew it, Rosie was standing inside the chapel itself. She gazed up the aisle at the simple but elegant wooden cross behind the pulpit, the emptiness of the place making her feel more at home than a full house ever would have. Sliding into a pew in the back, she sat back and soaked up the atmosphere.

Rosie had always believed in God—a belief that hadn't lessened just because she'd found out that she was a witch. To her way of thinking there was more than enough mysticism associated with each belief, and the two weren't mutually exclusive. But she didn't think she necessarily needed to be a Church-goer to be able to converse with the Almighty, either.

The irony of her thoughts made her laugh without humor. She relaxed back on her seat, letting her feeling of restlessness seep away. Her tension went with it, and for the first time in well over a week, Rosie managed to relax. It seemed to have been the only energy keeping her going. Before long, she found she was getting sleepy.

"Rosie?"

A warm hand shook her shoulder gently, causing her to stir and sit up quickly. Myles was standing in the aisle next to her, his face full of concern. "Are you alright?"

Lord—had she *really* fallen asleep in Church?

"I'm fine," she mumbled, blinking hard to push the sleepy feeling out of her eyes.

"Forgive me for sayin' so," he smiled softly, "but

you don't exactly *look* fine. I don't normally see you here. Not that I'm complainin'," he added pointedly.

"Guess I just needed somewhere to gather my thoughts," Rosie said sheepishly. "Didn't realize I also needed to catch some Z's."

"I get that," Myles nodded with a chuckle. He slipped into the pew beside her, his casual jeans and t-shirt reminding her that he was her friend as well as her Pastor. "I find it quite peaceful here, especially during the week like this."

"That's not the problem," Rosie shrugged, disheartened to be thinking about her problem *again.* "I'm gonna have *too much* peace. Maggie left for boarding school this morning."

Her throat felt tight, and she tried to take a deep breath to stop her emotions from welling over. She was successful, but not before Myles had noticed the turning of the tide.

"I'm sorry," he said softly, turning to face her properly.

"It's okay," she sighed, taking another deep breath.

"Well, not yet," Myles told her, "but it will be. I know it might not seem like that right now, and I know you won't stop missin' her while she's gone. But this too shall pass." He paused, looking at her thoughtfully. "Maybe you can help it pass more pleasantly."

Rosie was sure that there could be no way of making missing her daughter into a pleasant experience. "How's that?" she asked, trying not to sound sullen.

"Well," Myles smiled ruefully, and settled back on the pew. "I know from bein' a parent myself that there's *always* a million things that you put off because your focus is on the kids." He shrugged, lifting his hands for emphasis. "What about Nourish? With Maggie at school, you'll have extra time you can spend gettin' everything ready to open. You can spend more time in your garden. You can also spend more time with friends —it goes without sayin' that you're always welcome here, or at my place. I know the same goes for Tammy and Ben."

At least working on all the things she'd been putting off to work with Maggie on her magic would give her something else to think about. Moping wasn't going to get her anywhere fast.

"I hadn't thought about the time as an opportunity. I guess I was stuck on thinking about it as a void," she admitted.

"Perspective is a powerful tool," Myles said knowingly, nodding.

"It sure is," Rosie agreed. She glanced at Myles out of the corner of her eye, taking in his thoughtful expression and the way he had relaxed with her while still remaining attentive. "Tammy's lucky to have you, Myles," Rosie said, smiling at him. "The whole town is, really."

He blushed, the pinkening of his cheeks suddenly making the darkness of his hair and the blueness of his eyes less harsh than they might have looked otherwise.

"Nah," he said, shaking his head in disbelief. "I think *I'm* lucky to have *Tammy.*"

Suddenly and very clearly, Rosie had a vision of Myles holding out an absolutely stunning white gold engagement ring. She felt a burst of love in her heart, and it was all she could do to not leap into the air and cry with joy for her two wonderful friends.

"Good," Rosie grinned at him instead. She pushed her personal sadness to one side and leaning forward to place an airy, sisterly kiss on his cheek. She stood, straightened her shirt, and hoisted her purse. "Thanks Myles. You've really given me something to think about."

He stood up, too, his hands finding the pockets of his jeans. "Happy to help."

"I gotta go," Rosie smiled, backing away from him towards the door. "Seems like I'm busy, all of a sudden."

"See that you stay that way," he told her, faking seriousness.

"Yes, sir," Rosie teased, before turning. As she made her way out of the chapel, she saw a brochure stand in the foyer. She stopped to look at them, and when she saw a brochure about the counselling service Ben had mentioned, she picked one up and tucked it into her purse.

CHAPTER 16

Rosie marched back to Fox Cottage with a single purpose burning in the forefront of her mind. Now that Maggie was away at school and the COW was off her back, it was time to deal with the enormous rabbit pen in her yard. She didn't even bother going inside to put away her purse, opting instead to go straight to what she viewed as the beginning of all this grief.

"Right," she said forcefully, once she was standing in front of the pen she had conjured. Hundreds of briars and roots stood placidly before her, completely non-reactive to her can-do attitude. Rosie kept speaking to them anyway. "Y'all came from magic, and you're just gonna have to go right on back to... *wherever*," she told them.

She gathered her magic, pulling from the woods around her small backyard as though instinctively knowing she would need back up. When she had tried to use magic on the rabbits before, it hadn't worked. But maybe she needed to take her own advice and pour her love into the spell. For such a long time, Rosie had been all about trying to be the best mother she could be. Her love for herself—and who she was outside of being a parent—had fallen down her list of priorities.

But that was all set to change now. She thought about how making the hard decision to let Maggie go away to school had given her the opportunity to be resilient, and how she loved herself for being strong enough to let go. She felt a fierce admiration for the part of herself that dreamed of building her plant business, and for having the guts to strive for a career even though she didn't have any experience with anything other than part-time work. And lastly, she found the pride she had in herself for raising such a thoughtful, loving child with oodles of potential.

She let her energy steep in those emotions, soaking them up until she felt as though she was ready to start moving on with the future. And then she let her magic flow—not slowly, and steadily as she usually would, but in a big forceful gust the way *Maggie* might.

The spell boomed like a crash of thunder, making the trees shake. A strong wind surged from behind Rosie, bulldozing everything in its path. Rosie stumbled forward and caught her balance, but the makeshift pen she'd made wasn't so lucky. The roots and twigs that made up the fencing retreated back into the ground. The magic rode on the air, continuing through the woods, pushing through the trees like a bomb had gone off. The trees bounced back, but the pen didn't.

Rosie instantly felt lighter, as though the weight of those rabbits had been pressing on her. She gave an almost negligent-seeming wave of one hand, and the lawn grew back over the bare patch where the pen had been. Within the span of ten minutes all traces of the rabbits had vanished from her life.

All, that is, except for the fact that Maggie hadn't been there to see the magic at work.

Thinking of Maggie reminded Rosie of her unsecured fairy tree. Maybe it was time to pay Carol-Ann a little visit.

She borrowed Declan's truck, and about ten minutes later she swung around the bend as she pulled onto Oak Street. Her mission took her into a part of Mosswood she hadn't visited before—the narrow residential streets behind the Elementary School. She supposed this was where most of Maggie's friends would live, and as she passed the small rectangular houses that all looked as though they had been built from the same architectural plans, Rosie reminded herself of how lucky they were to be cozied up in Fox Cottage.

Rosie pulled up outside one of the cookie-cutter houses. This one was different to all the rest in that it had a smaller version of Rosie's own oak tree in the middle of its lawn, closer to the house and surrounded by a bed of cheerful daffodils. Steeling herself, Rosie jumped out of the truck. Her plan was simple: get in, secure the tree, and get out. Whatever 'secure the tree' meant.

She walked quickly across the lawn, her eyes darting left and right in a bid to avoid any nosy neighbors who might be watching the street. By the time she actually reached the tree she was none the wiser about how to tackle the spell, but time was of the essence. The last thing she needed was to get caught hanging around the front yard of her realtor's house.

Carol-Ann didn't strike her as the type of woman who should be messed with.

Rosie stepped up to the tree and placed her palms against the trunk, feeling more with her magic than her hands. A faint pulse fluttered beneath her touch, confirming to Rosie that this was indeed the tree that was a portal to the fairy tree in her own yard. Better to be safe than sorry.

She took a long, slow breath, gathering her magical energy. As she did she leaned slightly to the side, one eye trained on the front windows and porch. All was quiet on the western front—*for now*. Turning back to the task at hand Rosie began to push her magic outwards, letting it flow through her fingertips and into the tree itself.

The sound of the screen door creaking open squeezed a gasp out of her.

Carol-Ann came out onto her porch, arms crossed

and expression unimpressed. She lifted her chin at the tree.

"If you really think you can undo near two-hundred-year-old magic, you're more arrogant than I thought."

"Carol-Ann!" Rosie yelped in surprise. "I can explain. I—"

"Think you know better than Moira did?" Carol-Ann cut her off, a little of her sourness melting. "You definitely got her blood in ya, Lord knows."

The force of the revelation nearly had Rosie laid out on the dirt beside the daffodils she'd ruined. She reeled, holding one hand out to steady herself against the trunk of the oak tree. "*What?*"

Carol-Ann shrugged off-handedly. "Why don't you come in, have something to drink." She nodded. "This ain't porch-yelling conversation."

Stepping into Carol-Ann's house was like stepping into another world. It was nothing like the almost clinical decor of her realtor's office in town—a jewel-toned patchwork velvet couch and squishy looking armchairs greeted them as they passed through the living room, and the strong scent of pachouli incense followed them though the house. The woman walked barefoot on mis-matched vintage rugs ahead of Rosie, taking her straight out onto the back porch.

"Might as well get comfortable," Carol-Ann told her, gesturing to some wicker chairs around a small table. "You're gonna be here a while. Sit, while I fetch."

She disappeared back into the house, reemerging a

few moments later with a tray holding a jug of tea, glasses, and a plate of pastries. She began to serve.

"Thanks," Rosie said briefly, taking her glass of tea. Her attention was fixed on Carol-Ann, and now that she was so close to being able to ask the questions that had been burning in her mind since the door opened to Carol-Ann's lawn. "How do you know about all this?" she asked.

Carol-Ann laughed as she poured the tea. It was a dry, wheezy sort of laugh that sounded like it had been kept in mothballs. "Get straight to the point, don't ya," she smirked. "No beatin' around the bush. I like that. Never was much for small talk myself. Moira was the charmer."

Rosie's heart skipped a beat at the mention of her ancestor. "You know about Moira?"

"*About* her? Bless your heart." Carol-Ann took her own glass of tea and settled onto the chair opposite Rosie. "I knew *her*."

Rosie's eyes widened, but Carol-Ann gave such a serene nod that she was silenced, hopeful and waiting.

"I was alone when I first moved to Mosswood," Carol-Ann began, her gaze turning unfocused as though she was looking back through memories. "And I came here bent on fixin' that. Where I came from, folks always had somethin' to say about me. That I was strange—uncanny. I had dreams, you see."

She brushed imaginary crumbs from her dress, smoothing it down over her knees. "Dreams that came true, more often than not. When those dreams were good ones, people didn't seem to mind it so much. Innocent predictions, they would say, and laugh it off. But then I had a dream that the local crops would fail. And then I dreamed that the cows would give sour milk. Then I dreamed that all babies born within that same year would be stillborn." Her voice petered off, lost in her wry expression. "Folks didn't think my predictions were so innocent after all that. So, I came here, thinkin' to start fresh."

"Just like me," Rosie suggested, feeling an unexpected kinship for the woman sitting across from her.

"Just like *Moira*," Carol-Ann corrected her. "She wasn't just a breath of fresh air, she was a damn whirlwind. It didn't take me long to figure out that there was more to her than most people knew, and I felt a kinship to that. We became fast friends, she and I."

Rosie sipped her tea quietly, hanging on the other woman's every word.

"Eventually, she confided in me. Told me about her family, and how she came to be so far from home herself. She had Samuel already, of course. And by the time little Violet came along, she asked me to be the godmother."

Carol-Ann smiled wistfully, as though she still longed for those simpler times. "Most important role I ever filled on this earth, I don't mind saying. But I had a void inside of me," she added, her smile turning acidic.

"One that can't be filled, 'cept with becoming a mother myself. It wasn't meant to be—my dreams had already told me that long before I arrived in Mosswood. But I wasn't gettin' any younger, and I feared dying alone. And that's when Moira made me her bargain."

A witch's pact. A binding, Rosie thought, her eyebrows rising. She held her breath.

"Just like Fabien," Rosie murmured, the pieces falling into place.

Carol-Ann nodded with approval. "I see you've been to Savannah. Moira gave me the duty of being the protector of her line, the royal line of the Kelly witches. We completed the ritual while Violet was still a baby, just in case anything should happen."

"But..." Rosie began, mentally doing the math. "If you knew Moira, you would have to be—"

"Now it ain't polite to ask a lady her age," Carol-Ann sniffed. "Suffice to say that I have seen more years than any mortal woman ever should."

Rosie took a moment to process everything. Had this woman been able to help her this whole time, and just never bothered to say anything? Rosie's temper sparked. "Why didn't you just *say* something?"

"Couldn't." Carol-Ann said in the blunt way Rosie was already becoming accustomed to. "Wasn't allowed."

"Wasn't allowed by who?" Rosie demanded. "The COW? Did they send you to spy on me?"

Carol-Ann seemed confused. "The COW?"

"The Council," Rosie clarified, hating the way the word felt in her mouth.

"Oh," the other woman nodded, before rolling her eyes again. "*Those* idiots. I haven't had anything to do with them in years."

"Then why?" Rosie asked.

"Because Moira didn't want anyone interfering in the lives of her descendants the way her parents had interfered in hers," she explained. "It was all part of the magic, and if I'd broken my promise—"

"You'd have been stuck," Rosie finished, and Carol-Ann finished the thought.

"And I wouldn't have been able to protect anyone."

"So, Moira died, and you stayed in your human form," Rosie prompted, "and you've been living in Mosswood all these years?"

"Yes ma'am," Carol-Ann drawled, holding up her tea in a cheers before taking a sip.

"But the plant you brought to the was dead," Rosie began before she was interrupted. "Why didn't you just fix it with magic yourself?"

"—was a test," Carol-Ann said, hastily swallowing an ice cube she had been meaning to crunch, "I had no reason to interfere while it seemed like things were progressing well. But then I heard the Council had been to see you."

"So, you just let me fail in front of the Council without telling me about your fairy tree?" Rosie asked, annoyed.

"Sorry about it," Carol-Ann shrugged, not looking sorry at all. "I've been sworn to protect you and your bloodline. I'm not about to give up now."

Rosie stared, trying to understand. "Getting me in trouble with the Council was protecting me?" she asked.

Carol-Ann knitted her brows together and looked at her sharply. "Don't be slow, girl. I wasn't protecting you from being Lost." She sat up a little straighter and nodded her chin once, with finality. "I was protecting you from being found."

Rosie narrowed her eyes suspiciously. "Do you know what happened to my parents, Carol-Ann?" she asked, her jaw set. She didn't know if she was prepared for the conversation, but she just had to ask.

"I do," Carol-Ann said grimly.

Rosie felt her breath catch in her throat, like she'd suddenly been thrown in the middle of a huge, ice-cold lake. That water had been murky for so damn long that she didn't know if dredging it now would be a good thing or a bad one. But her heart ached, and she needed to *know*.

She met Carol-Ann's gaze, folding her hands in her lap to keep them steady. "Tell me."

"Your parents were researching their family history and found information that led them to Moira—which brought them here," Carol-Ann began, leaning back in her chair as though settling in for the tale. "I had Moira's diary, which I gave to your mother—Moira's heir. Your parents decided to settle into Fox Cottage and use it as a base to learn more about your heritage, but exposing your mother to Moira's magic stirred an ancient evil. One that coveted Moira's magic and wanted to absorb it."

Carol-Ann looked directly into Rosie's eyes. "Wizards."

The word sent an electric shock through Rosie's memory as she thought back to the few instances when Declan had mentioned the other magical faction. Carol-Ann took her wide-eyed astonishment as a signal to move on with the story.

"I knew your folks needed more help than I could provide. So, I did what I thought was best... at the time."

"You put them in touch with the Council," Rosie breathed.

Carol-Ann gave a small shrug. "The magic that binds me to Moira is finite. They needed help with magic in ways I couldn't ever begin to understand. But we were too late. It became too dangerous for your parents to remain in Mosswood, and impossible for them to protect you. I helped them find a foster home to take you in where the wizards wouldn't find you. Moira's magic called for the protection of her line—the three of us were bound to secrecy about your location. And you..."

The older woman drifted off for a moment, her face softening at the memory of a tiny baby who had been left all alone in the world. "Bless your heart, even as a baby you must have known what you were facin'. You seemed to suppress your own magic, almost like you thought that was why your parents gave you up."

Rosie's heart was racing. She had always hoped that there was more to her abandonment than just being unwanted—that there was some really good reason her parents had just left her to fend for herself in a world that was often too cruel. She took a breath and frowned. "But wouldn't I have just been bound by the same protection magic that bound you all?"

Carol-Ann shook her head. "No, child. While your mother was in Mosswood, her powers bloomed. I thought it was a sign that she was coming into her own, that she was the heir in line to inherit all of Moira's power and be Queen." She smiled, a sad but hopeful smile that tore at Rosie's heart. "But it was because she was carryin' *you*. Your magic is so powerful that only you could lock it away, keep yourself safe. And once you felt that you were worthy of bein' loved again..."

"...my magic came back," Rosie finished. She let this new knowledge sit with her for a moment, turning it over and over in her mind as she tried to fit all the pieces of the puzzle together.

She sighed, leaning forward to rest her elbows on her knees. "So, why are you allowed to tell me all this now?" she asked then.

Carol-Ann hesitated and then spoke calmly. "'Cause my time protecting the Kelly bloodline is comin' to an end." Rosie's breath whooshed out of her, but Carol-

Ann continued. "When you fulfill the prophecy, my part of the bargain will be done."

"So, you do your job and your reward is that you'll die?" Rosie asked, horrified.

Carol-Ann laughed. "I know it don't make much sense to a young thing like you." *Young?* Rosie thought, but didn't dare argue with someone who had more gray hair than she did. Carol-Ann continued. "I've had more families, raised more kids, seen more summers than most people ever do. I learned a long time ago what Moira meant for me to learn. A family doesn't have to be your own blood to be yours."

Rosie felt her cheeks warm. She'd never known, growing up, that she had family out there all the while, but she knew exactly what Carol-Ann was talking about because she'd chosen her family in Mosswood just the same.

Carol-Ann nodded slowly. "Moira kept her end of the bargain. I'm happy to keep mine. So here goes, Rosie Bell."

She leaned forward and took one of Rosie's hands between her two.

"You're a Queen. That's part mother, part protector, and you represent it for every magical person who was ever outcast or banished or left behind. There's no one who can make up your mind for you or force you any which way but your own." She sat up a little and let go of Rosie's hand.

"You're in the most dangerous part, now," she

continued. "They know about ya, now, and they'll be trying to control you." She shook her head. "Don't let 'em. You and that little girl of yours, you do what's best for you. And if you can manage to do that, you'll be the Queen the rest of us need."

She let her shoulders settle around her like a mantle of power. "That's all I need to say. The rest is up to you."

Rosie thought about what Carol-Ann had to say. She was bolstered by the wise woman's words, but knew deep down that she still had a long way to go. She looked up at her advisor and tilted her head.

"Carol-Ann? What's your familiar form?"

"Oh," she waved the question away, "That don't matter."

Rosie's suspicion was instantly piqued. "Why not?" she asked.

Carol-Ann continued, "Well, because, I—" She stopped her hemming and hawing and looked Rosie in the eye.

"It's a skunk."

For a moment, Rosie didn't think anything of it except the strangeness of the choice, but then the combination of Carol-Ann's embarrassment and the animal form she took drew a connection in her memory.

"Oh, no," she said.

"Oh, yes," Carol-Ann replied matter-of-factly.

"Oh, crap."

"Well, honey, you look better in your birthday suit

than I do."

"Oh, *God*."

Rosie was never looking at any animal the same way again.

Her hot cheeks told her that it was time for a change of subject. She shook her head. "How would the wizards have known where my parents were? Are we still in danger?"

"Beats me," Carol-Ann said with a frown that spoke volumes on her opinion of wizards. "Nasty S.O.B.'s, with their dead black eyes. Oh, they're better at hidin' it these days of course, but trust me—in my time, that was a clear sign! Thankfully, Moira's magic is such that it gives us the ability to see that trick. She knew who was huntin' her."

Full and utter paralysis threatened to take Rosie over. All she could see in her mind was Morgan's flat black eyes, so shark-like, so predatory. Every hair on her body felt like it stood on end, and she leaned forward to support herself on the table.

"What is it?" Carol-Ann asked, surprised.

"Morgan," Rosie gasped. "On the Council! She has those eyes!"

Carol-Ann's eyes widened with horror. "So *that's* how the wizards found your parents! They had a spy within the Council itself!"

Rosie didn't care about how they had found her parents. There was only one thing on her mind. "And now they have my daughter."

CHAPTER 17

Rosie and Carol-Ann had abandoned the sweet tea and thrown themselves into Declan's truck, rumbling through town and up The Ridge as fast as they dared. Pulling up with a skid on the gravel that was enough to tempt Declan out of the house, Rosie tumbled out of the truck and ran to him.

"Whoa," he said, alarmed. "Where's the fire?"

"It's Maggie," Rosie huffed, in no mood for jokes. "Morgan's a wizard, and she's got Maggie alone at that school. We have to go get her! We have to—"

Declan's eyes widened, and he looked from Rosie to Carol-Ann and back again. "How d'ya know Morgan's a wizard?"

"I saw her eyes!" Rosie said frantically. "We can talk about that later, okay? Right now we—"

Rosie was interrupted by the sound of her cell ringing in her back pocket. She snatched the phone out, and almost cried with relief when she saw the number of Greybriar Academy on the screen. She fumbled hastily to take the call, swiping her finger across the screen.

"Maggie!?" she asked, her voice thick with panic.

"—om, I'm ju—" Maggie said on the other end of the line, her voice broken up by static.

"Maggie, are you okay?" Rosie asked, desperately pressing the phone closer to her ear as though it would help her to hear better.

"—ome for me—" Maggie continued. "I didn't— they were wiz—"

Rosie's blood froze in her veins. "Get back in the truck," she said, breaking into a run and tossing the keys back to Declan. "We're going there right now. She's saying something about wizards, but I can't hear her. We need to get there *now!*" She kept running. "Maggie? Mags, can you hear me hon? We're on our way!"

The three of them began to run for the truck, not noticing the breeze that had suddenly whipped up around them. It tugged at Rosie's ponytail, making it stream behind her as she made for the truck. It wasn't until she pulled the door open and looked back at Declan and Carol-Ann that Rosie noticed the wind was only in the space surrounding the fairy tree. And then she let out a cry of relief that made Carol-Ann and Declan stop in their tracks.

Maggie stumbled out of the door in the fairy tree, her dark curls wild and free in the wind. She looked around the lawn as though searching for something, and when she saw Rosie she broke into a full sprint.

Rosie did the same. Her legs couldn't get her across the small divide and to her daughter fast enough for her liking. They came together into a crashing hug, and Rosie held Maggie so tightly that it was a wonder the poor kid could breathe at all.

"Mom!" Maggie gasped. "I'm so glad you're here! I was so scared! These crazy people with black eyes came right for me while I was just hanging out with my new friends—they tried to grab me!"

"What happened?" Rosie asked, holding Maggie at arm's length so that she could see her precious little face. "How did you get here? Are they following you?"

"I used the fairy tree you gave me. I guess its magic was stronger than we thought! And I don't think so?" Maggie grinned cheekily. "I turned them into turtles."

Carol-Ann blinked. "How many?"

"Three," Maggie said, looking from Carol-Ann to her Mom in confusion as though wondering whether or not the hawkish older woman was to be trusted.

"If she can turn three fully-fledged wizards into turtles at the mere age of nine—" Carol-Ann said, trailing off with an expression that betrayed how impressed she was.

"I'm nearly 11!" Maggie protested.

"—even so," Carol-Ann added. "It shows that her magic's far beyond anythin' we could have been prepared for."

Maggie glanced at Carol-Ann again. "Mom?"

"It's fine hon," Rosie said, rubbing Maggie's shoulder. "Carol-Ann's helping us. She knew Moira."

It was Maggie's turn to be impressed, though whether it was by Carol-Ann's age or her connections was anyone's guess. "Wow," she breathed, as Carol-Ann offered her a tight smile.

"I hate to interrupt," Declan said, his voice tinged with urgency. "But we have company."

Another strong wind blew up around the yard, just like the one that blew when the Council first appeared on her lawn. Rosie pulled Maggie closer as three puffs of magical smoke in different colors burst into existence, and the Council came striding out of them over to where the others stood. Cillian's face was an unreadable as ever, but Morgan looked almost white-faced with rage while Hella sauntered behind them both with a smirk.

"I should have known that any child of Moira's line would be incapable of abiding by Council rules," Morgan called as they approached. "I suppose she sold you some childish story about being attacked," she laughed coldly, "on Greybriar grounds, no less?"

Rosie straightened, looking Morgan right in her lifeless black eyes.

"I believe every word," she said, squaring her shoulders, "because I know exactly what you are. *Wizard.*"

Hella's hands flew to her brightly-lipsticked mouth

as she let out a horrified, and more than slightly melodramatic gasp.

"Preposterous!" Morgan snarled, a darkly amused expression on her rounded face. "What a ridiculous accusation! This disrespect will not be tolerated!" She turned to Cillian, as though expecting him to back her up. But he was looking at Rosie, his face growing paler by the second.

"What makes ya think she's a wizard?" he asked.

"Well, y'all can't see it, but her eyes are blacker'n her soul," Carol-Ann interjected, "or lack, thereof."

Morgan rounded on her. "Funny you should be so concerned about that, *servant*," she growled, "When you sold yours for a pittance."

Carol-Ann narrowed her eyes one hand lifting to rest ominously on her bony hip.

Cillian was looking across Morgan at Hella, as though they were speaking silently. He jutted his chin in Morgan's direction. Hella nodded.

She waved a hand in Morgan's direction, binding her with thin strips of bright orange light.

"What do you think you're doing?!" Morgan screeched, struggling against her magical bonds. "This is out of order!"

"Maybe," Cillian said slowly, "but you'll forgive us, if it turns out you have nothin' to hide."

"Argh!!" Morgan cried, bending forward. She summoned her own magical energy and as she straightened, she pushed her arms out against the binding spell that Hella had constructed around her. The magical strips of light began to pop as they snapped, freeing her.

"Oh no the hell she *don't*," Hella said, adopting a fighting stance.

Cillian looked at Declan. "Make ya'self useful," he snapped. "Grab her!"

"Grab her?" Morgan blinked, an incredulous look spreading over her pale face. "*Grab her?*" She began to laugh, the sound bubbling up in her throat as the witches slowly began to surround her. "You may be descended from Merlin, Cillian, but you will never match him for power." She looked down her nose disparagingly at Cillian and sniffed disdainfully. "And if he couldn't stop me, you surely won't."

A dark expression of realization settled onto Cillian's face. "You'll find a *lot* has changed, *Morgana*," he snarled, pushing up his sleeves before clapping his hands together, hard, to energize them.

"Indeed, it has," Morgana purred, running a hand down her pin-striped secretary skirt to smooth it out. "But the frailty of witches never will."

She lifted both of her arms in sync, like a bird preparing to take flight. When both arms were above her head she brought them down in front of her, her fingers sizzling with power that she levelled straight at Cillian.

He was ready for her. As the jet of red light streaked towards him he placed one foot in front of the other, bracing for it. Rosie's heart was in her throat as Cillian whispered something, and the red magic hit an invisible protection spell he had conjured at the last minute. Morgana's spell melted away, and a loud boom shook the trees in the woods around Fox Cottage as Cillian shot a bolt of bright blue magic back at her with impressive speed and accuracy.

In a move that mocked Cillian's blockage of her spell, Morgana brushed her hand aside as though shooing a fly. "Pathetic," she sighed, lifting a hand as she pretended to inspect her nails. "There's no wonder your line is a laughing-stock."

Declan bristled. "He's a *King*. Show some respect!"

"Wizards *have* no respect. Stay out of this, lad," Cillian told his son, his hands held low and his eyes on Morgana.

"You'd better do as Daddy says," Morgana grinned wickedly.

Declan's eyes widened, pursing his lips and lifting his hands as his temper got the better of him.

"Declan," Cillian shouted. "*No!*"

But it was too late—Declan had already loosed his spell. He didn't fight with fire. His chosen magic glittered and cracked as it shot through the air in a frosty blur. As it passed her and Maggie, Rosie could feel the depth of the chill that accompanied it, noticing the needle-like shards of ice that sought to plunge themselves into Morgana.

Cillian turned his attention to his son as soon as Declan's spell was in the air, bringing one closed fist to his heart before throwing it outwards in his son's direction. The same invisible disturbance he had used before rippled through the air with a dull *wud-wud-wud* sound until it surrounded Declan. It disappeared then, but Rosie knew that Cillian had just cast a protection spell over his son.

Rosie spun, pulling Maggie closer and placing both her hands on her daughter's head. Her magic was different to Cillian's—she didn't know any fancy forcefield spells that she could cast to keep *her* kid safe. But she planned on doing whatever she *could*. Maggie looked up at her with wide, frightened eyes and Rosie gently pushed her magic out, forming it into an invisible skin that would cover Maggie like a protective cocoon.

"Listen to me," Rosie told her. "I need you to—"

But before Rosie could finish her sentence, a bright red flash of light burst into her peripheral vision.

"Mom!" Maggie cried out, raising her own hand. A surge of magic detonated, sending a shower of bright pink sparks over the both of them as she deflected Morgana's spell. Rosie looked at her in awe.

"Protect yourself, too," Maggie told her, lifting her chin bravely.

Rosie began to move in Morgana's direction, but the wizard was too busy to sass her. Cillian, Hella, and Declan all had their focus trained on her, shooting spell after spell. While it was clear that she was more powerful magically than any one of them, she was having a hard time keeping up with attacks on three fronts.

Cillian's face twisted into a grimace, as he forced his magic from his hands in a sudden burst of lime-green light. It sizzled through the air, looking for all the world like poison in lightning form. Morgana only just managed to side-step it, but not before it singed the hem of her skirt. She smirked triumphantly, until a dark blue bolt of energy caught her squarely in the middle of the back. She howled with pain, contorting to look over her shoulder at Hella who gave her a feminine wave.

"Oh hey, *bitch*," the tiny drag queen snapped.

Morgana didn't waste any time. She threw her own magic at Hella, but it was nothing like the kind of magic Rosie had seen witches use. This magic looked like little more that shadows shifting through the air, full of toxic smoke and sparks of dark red embers burning brightly as it sought its target.

Hella wasn't ready. The magic struck her in the chest, knocking her flat to the ground.

"No!" Rosie cried, gathering her energy up as she ran forward. Morgana felt the changing of the atmosphere and glanced over her shoulder at Rosie with a vicious, hungry smile.

"That's right," she purred. "Leave little Magnolia there and come and play with the big kids. When I've finished with your four, she'll be there waiting for me." Her eyes flicked to Maggie. "Won't you, sweetheart?"

"Yeah," Maggie shot back defiantly. "Waiting to finish you off!"

"You sweet little thing," Morgana chuckled. "That's just the spirit I admire in you. None of *my* daughters had that kind of fire. Or at least, not until I took their bodies."

Rosie felt sick as the implication of Morgana's words filled her brain. She had been using the bodies of her daughters for centuries, skipping from one to the next in a demented hop-scotch to try and maintain immortality? It was horrifying. She would *never* do that her daughter.

Cillian paled. "You play a dangerous game, Morgana," he warned her. "That kind of necromancy often leaves a soul wandering the earth for eternity."

"Immortality combined with unstoppable power," Morgana mused. "What could be better?"

With that, she vanished into thin air just as Myles had seen her do the last time she had been at Fox Cottage. She reappeared a split-second later, standing behind Maggie with one hand curled around the child's throat.

Maggie immediately began to struggle. "Mom!"

"Maggie!" Rosie yelled starting to run even as everyone else started to move as well.

"One step closer and I'll snap her pretty little neck," Morgana warned sharply.

She meant it. Rosie froze in place, her heart racing.

Morgana slowly let her attention ease from Rosie to Maggie.

"I can't wait to try this raw power on for size," she purred, stroking Maggie's neck. "It'll be like slipping into a crystal-infused spring in summer. *So* refreshing," Morgana sighed, clearly already imagining her victory. She bent closer to Maggie's face, her eyes returning to Rosie's. "So sweet."

Rosie watched Morgana inching closer to Maggie, feeling her blood pressure rising with every second. She'd be damned if she was going to let some power-hungry ancient *whoever* anywhere near her baby girl. It was time to channel her inner Sigourney Weaver.

"Get away from her, you *bitch*," Rosie growled.

There was a long, ominous rumble in the sky above them. The wind that had been rustling the fairy tree intensified as the roots of Moira's nearby Irish magic were pulled into the force Rosie conjured. And then she unleashed the full force of that magic.

Morgana looked up just in time to see a huge bolt of lightning break through the sudden cloudbank above them. It lit up the whole sky even though it was the middle of the day, crackling with ferocity as it plummeted downwards to strike her upturned face. Morgana pushed Maggie out of the way to take the brunt of the hit herself.

Rosie ran back to Maggie, holding her close. Declan joined them a moment later.

"Holy *shit*," Declan breathed, gazing with awe at Rosie. "That was *amazin'!*"

Cillian watched her with typical unreadable expression. "I've never seen anythin' like that," he told her, which in his terms was tantamount to straight out praise. "But we're not finished yet," he added grimly, walking over to where Morgana lay writhing in the dirt.

Carol-Ann had run over to Hella and was helping her slowly to her feet.

Morgana cackled—a dark, harrowing sound that was punctuated by the blood that kept bubbling up through her lips.

"Kill me," she laughed, looking up at Cillian with her real, crazed black eyes that were blurred from the pain caused by the lightning.

Cillian really looked for a moment as though he might do just that. And then he backed off. "Ya not worth it," he hissed at her.

"What will you do, then?" She grinned, blood staining her teeth. "You can't kick me off the Council. I earned my seat."

"You manipulated your way onto the Council through centuries of lies and bloodshed," he growled. "I know the old tales, *wizard*. I'll see to it that you're banished from the Council."

"I *invented* banishing," Morgana snarked with a wet-sounding laugh. "Just like I made *you,* Cillian Forrest! You're nothing without the Council, and the Council is nothing without *me!*"

Cillian leaned down, his ordinarily steely resolve slipping as disgust and rage filled his face. "The Council was born before you, and it will endure *after* you," Cillian spat, his temper flaring again. A surge of energy flooded the air around him, fluctuating wildly.

"Go on," she urged him. "*Kill me.* I can feel your desire to do it, Cillian. It would feel *so good*, wouldn't it?"

Cillian drew more energy, building a force.

Rosie felt a familiar chill travelling through her body. She didn't know exactly what it meant, until the chill reached her heart.

"*DO IT!*" Morgana screamed.

"No!" Rosie cried. She rushed forward, grabbing Cillian's forearm. "That's what she *wants.*" She looked into Morgana's black eyes. "What did you do to my daughter?"

Morgana laughed again, but it was weaker. "Kill me," she said, her voice husky from shouting and dropping to a whisper. "And find out."

Rosie couldn't blame Cillian for wanting to end Morgana. She wanted the honors herself. But she refused to play that game. Cillian was still coiled like a snake waiting to strike, and Rosie didn't know how she could talk him down off a ledge she was half occupying herself.

And then Maggie was there. She slipped quietly through the group of adults, pushing past Rosie before she could be stopped. Her little hand found Cillian's tightly closed fist, and with the persistence and charm that only a child possessed, she wriggled her small fingers underneath his until he loosened his hand and it covered hers.

"Don't listen to her, Grandpa," she said calmly, ignoring Morgana all but incapacitated on the ground beside them. "She's looking for the easy way. Don't give it to her." Maggie began to tug Cillian backwards, breaking his focus on Morgana until he had to take a step backwards. His head bowed and he leaned down into a quick, almost-embarrassed hug with Maggie. When he straightened Rosie could see the tears that were shining, unshed, in his eyes.

"Fools," Morgana croaked. "How very like Merlin's ancestors, to leave unfinished business free to haunt them."

With that, Morgana clear vanished in front of all of them. They all looked around, searching for some sign that she was still nearby. Finding none, they regrouped.

"Are ya alright, Da'?" Declan asked, approaching his father.

"I'm sorry, lad," Cillian said, his voice heavy with a sigh. "I didn't realize—what a bloody fool I've been!" He shook his head angrily. "For years, that soulless, foul thing has been right under my nose!" He pressed his lips together before clapping his son on the shoulder and looking him in the eye. "You were right."

"Hold on, let me record that," Declan grinned.

"You couldn't have known," Carol-Ann, said gently,

joining the group after double-checking the perimeter including the fairy tree. "They evolve, adapt to their circumstances." She pulled a face. "Like cockroaches."

Rosie hadn't let Maggie out of her sight. She sat a little way off with her, swinging on the porch swing and holding her child in a fierce embrace that was returned a hundred-fold.

"Gosh, I'm so damn happy to have you safe and sound," Rosie said against Maggie's soft, tousled curls.

"I'm so happy to *be* here safe and sound," Maggie said, already sounding older than she had before she'd gone away to school. *Lord.* It had only been a day!

"That happiness might be short lived," Cillian said, as he, Declan, Hella and Carol-Ann joined them. His expression was apologetic, as though he wanted to make amends as both a Council member *and* a member of the family. "I can't remove the Council's ultimatum for Maggie to be at school. I told ya before. Once the magic's set in place, it's final. If Maggie chooses to remain here, then you'll both be Lost by Banishment."

Rosie pressed her lips together and moved back, so that she could look into her daughter's eyes. Maggie looked back at her calmly, before a slow smile took hold of her lips.

"That's okay," Maggie declared firmly. "We're not *really* Lost. Not as long as we're together."

CHAPTER 18

The line of people out of the brightly painted pink door of Nourish was even bigger than the one they'd had when they'd sold off all of Terry's old hunting stock. The furniture inside had been hastily and temporarily re-arranged to allow for the number of customers, with Maggie and a few of her school friends occupying the largest table in the center of the room that had been too heavy to move just for a day. They drank soda out of plastic wine glasses and ate their lunches, gossiping about what all had been happening in their lives just the way grown women might do during a girls' lunch.

Rosie and Tammy watched them from behind the counter, and then smiled knowingly at each other. It had been a bit of a stretch to get everything organized to open the store on short notice, but now that they were there in the thick of things Rosie was so glad they'd made the effort. She'd already sold most of her plants, and Tammy's cooking was an absolute hit. The bright teal vintage coffee machine they'd managed to purchase for cheap hadn't stopped all day, and Myles showed off his unexpected barista skills as he kept them pumping out.

Declan bused the tables, a bright pink apron tied securely around his waist. He laughed and joked with customers, checking on those who had been served and entertaining those who hadn't. The atmosphere was electric, and by the time Ben moseyed in through the door Rosie could understand just why he was a bit of a workaholic. A day of successful business trading really felt quite addictive.

"Congratulations, ladies," he drawled, pleased as punch as he handed Rosie a huge bouquet of spring wildflowers.

"Oh Ben," Rosie sniffed them, then held them out for Tammy to do the same while her hands were busy plating up slices of cake. "These are gorgeous. You shouldn't have!"

"Why shouldn't I?" he grinned. "This is a huge day for y'all, and I'm so proud of you both. Just make sure you give me plenty of notice before you go quittin' on me, okay?" he teased.

"Thank you," Tammy told him, grabbing the plates and stepping around the counter to place a chaste kiss on Ben's cheek before turning back to Rosie mischievously. "Did Declan get you a 'congratulations' present?"

"Not yet," Declan cut in, carrying a stack of plates past them on a mission out back. He lowered his voice, leaning into the group. "But this pink apron might make a cameo tonight, if she's lucky." He left them all laughing as he ducked away again, just as a tiny woman in head-to-toe khaki approached the counter.

"Welcome to Nourish, Sheriff," Tammy greeted her chirpily. "So nice of you to stop on by on our first day."

The woman smiled broadly, glanced at Ben, and then nodded at Rosie. "Wouldn't miss it," she said, glancing at the menu on the counter. "Black coffee and a bear claw to go," she said. "No sugar."

"Is that 'cos you're already sweet enough?" Ben asked. Immediately after, his expression changed to one of embarrassment, as though he couldn't believe that he'd just said that.

The Sheriff's expression said that she couldn't believe he'd just said that, either. "No," she said simply. "It's because too much sugar gives me gas."

Rosie pressed her lips together to stop from laughing, and Tammy took that opportunity to deliver the plates she was holding to the customers who were waiting for them. A welcome distraction in the form of a bright green cab pulling up right outside the door turned all their heads in that direction.

"What the hell," the Sheriff muttered darkly, sighing. "Can't they read the one-way traffic sign off

Lee Street? All we need is for a delivery truck to come down the lane and clean that cab up. Ugh!" She started to make her way through the crowd towards the door.

The cab driver stepped out into the lane, allowing himself a well-earned stretch. Rosie could see that it was the same driver who had delivered her to Mosswood, and the same one who had brought Gemma. He was clearly the type of guy who didn't mind the extra-long fares. Leaving the cab parked squarely in the middle of the lane, he waddled into the store. When he spied Maggie with her plastic 'birthday girl' tiara on, he grinned.

"Hey! Happy birthday!" he declared, before helping himself to refreshments.

"Hey," the Sheriff told him in a no-nonsense tone, "you're parked illegally."

"Oh," the cabbie said, his face falling as he listened to the Sheriff's renewed lecture about the one-way status of the laneway.

The passenger in the back of the cab had unfolded himself and gotten out of the back door. He was a tall kid, around fourteen or so, with freckles and blonde hair. He pulled a suitcase behind him as he entered the store, and the cab took off the wrong way down the lane. The Sheriff threw her hands up in the air in defeat.

The kid started to approach the counter when Declan came hustling back onto the main floor. He was taking his newly appointed role as step-dad seriously and had baked the cake himself (even though Tammy had begged him repeatedly to take care of it). He carried a plate with a huge teal-colored birthday cake with eleven candles burning brightly on top over to Maggie's table.

"Haaaappy birthdaaaay to youuuu," he began to sing in a low voice.

The rest of the crowd in the shop heard him and turned to look before catching on and joining in.

"Happy birthday to you!"

Rosie grinned and walked with him towards Maggie, who was sitting up straighter at the table and watching her birthday cake approach with big, excited eyes.

"Happy biiiiirthday, dear Maggie," Rosie sang as Declan put the cake down on the table, holding up her hands to encourage more people to join in. "Haaaaaappy birthday to yoooooou!"

Maggie leaned forward, huffing to blow out all her candles. The crowd cheered, and she grinned.

Rosie couldn't believe that her baby was already eleven. The years were just flying by, and it was a good reminder to her that if she blinked, she might miss it. With a smile on her face, she noticed Carol-Ann standing just inside the door. Their eyes met—Carol-Ann smiled—and Rosie nodded in greeting. But then a movement to her right caught her eye.

Declan had ducked back to the kitchen to grab a knife and a stack of paper plates. The kid who had gotten out of the cab had been lingering near the counter, but now stepped directly into Declan's path.

Declan offered the kid an apologetic smile, and stepped to the other side, but the kid blocked him again. A small frown creased Declan's brow, as he obviously wondered what the kid's problem was. He studied the kid's face slowly, a look of horrified comprehension creeping onto his own face. And then the kid let go of his suitcase and crossed his arms.

"Hi, *Dad*," he sneered in a crisp British accent.

Thanks for reading

Thank you so much for reading the fourth instalment of my *Midlife in Mosswood* series - I hope you loved reading it as much and I loved writing it.

Being a mum is the toughest job I have ever had. It's a wild rollercoaster ride full of the highest highs, and the lowest lows. And while at times it's been incredibly tough, when I look at the incredible young woman my daughter is becoming I am overcome with pride.

Hold your loved ones a little closer. Every moment is precious.

Son of a Witch will be book five in the series, and promises a country wedding, a big catastrophe, and more laughs and love from your favourite people in Mosswood.

Until then, stay safe and take care of yourself.

Louisa xo

Bless your heart

Thank you to my very own Pumpkin, Elizabeth, who shows me so much love and support. Her ideas for Maggie are sprinkled throughout this book, and her artwork graces the cover and also gets page-time. Though she be but little, she is fierce—and I wouldn't have it any other way.

Thank you to my editor, Kimberly Jaye. As always, she is able to take the ramblings of my mind and help me repackage them until they're fit for human consumption. If that's not magic, then I don't know what is.

Thanks to my amazing partner, Lindsay, who once again dropped everything to read my latest book and proof-read it for me. Amidst the red dirt of the outback while he was away at work, no less!

Thank you to my mum, whose faith that a Netflix deal is just around the corner literally keeps me going.

Thanks again to my ARC team, who line up to read these books and tell me nice things about them. My gratitude knows no bounds!

Lastly… thank you so much to you. By reading this book, you're helping my lifelong dream continue to bloom and come to fruition. That makes us kin, in my mind. Welcome to the family.

Love it? Review it!

A reader writing a review for a book is such a gift to an author. Not only does it let us know that someone out there actually read the thing, but it's so heart-warming to think that they enjoyed it enough to offer their thoughts on it afterwards.

If you've enjoyed this book, I would be so grateful if you'd consider leaving me a review! You can do this by searching for the book title and my name on Amazon.com or on GoodReads and then following the prompts.

If you're a book-blogger, bookstagrammer, or journalist and you would like to interview me, please get in touch with me at www.louisawest.com - I would love to chat with you!

Your next Mosswood adventure awaits!

SON OF A
WITCH

MIDLIFE IN MOSSWOOD BOOK 5

Preorder now on Amazon and in Kindle Unlimited

https://books2read.com/sofaw

Son of a Witch

She knew she'd have to find something old and something new. This wasn't what she was expecting.

Rosemary Bell is going to the chapel and someone's gonna get married. But when an unexpected visitor begins causing trouble in Mosswood, the something blue on Tammy's big day could end up being the bride.

For better or worse, Fox Cottage has a new resident. And mostly, it's for worse. With Declan struggling to rein in his wayward son, Rosie ends up playing referee as well as bridesmaid--and she doesn't look good in stripes. Wanting to support her boyfriend and still keep peace in the neighborhood, Rosie is stuck between a diamond and a hard place.

When the teenage troublemakers commit a ceremony foul, will Rosie find herself one family richer or one group of friends poorer?

Freaky Friday meets *My Best Friend's Wedding* **in this short novel about the vows we make, the promises we break, and the things we do for family's sake.**

AVAILABLE JUNE 30 2021
PREORDER: https://books2read.com/sofaw

MIDLIFE IN
MOSSWOOD

PARANORMAL WOMEN'S FICTION SERIES

LOUISA WEST

Also by Louisa West

THE MIDLIFE IN MOSSWOOD SERIES

New Witch on the Block

https://books2read.com/nwotb

Jealousy's A Witch

https://books2read.com/jaw

We Witch You A Merry Christmas

https://books2read.com/wwyamc

Get Witch Quick

https://books2read/gwq

Son of a Witch

https://books2read/sofaw

About the author

Louisa likes Pina Coladas and gettin' caught in the rain. Determined to empty her brain of stories, she loves writing Paranormal Women's Fiction and other stories about kick-ass women doing whatever the hell they want to do.

She lives in Mandurah, Western Australia, and drinks more coffee than is good for her. When she's not writing or researching projects, Louisa enjoys spending time with her family, and Harriet The Great (Dane). Hobbies include playing video games, watching copious amounts of tv, and various craft-related initiatives.

She strongly believes that the truth is still out there.

Are you interested in:

- New release information and pre-order links
- Competitions, giveaways, and other freebies
- Sneak peeks at cover reveals and excerpts
- VIP access to online launch parties and
- Exclusive member rewards

Then join Louisa's online reader group at
www.facebook.com/groups/magicalmayhem!

facebook.com/louisawestauthor

instagram.com/louisa_west

amazon.com/author/louisawest

goodreads.com/louisawest

pinterest.com/louisawestauthor